This book is dedicated to the boundles   ̲ ̲ ̲my family, thank you. Carl, you've provid̲ ̲ ̲ ̲ ̲ ̲me with more inspiration than you'll ever know. And of course, to Ted.

I have taken great liberty with the names of streets, areas and locations. Whilst all can be found within the Huddersfield or Rochdale areas, I have amalgamated a few descriptions to maintain some anonymity, thus creating a few cross county hybrids.

All characters appearing in this work are fictitious. Any resemblance to real persons, living or dead, is purely coincidental.

Black Matter

Chapter One

It was an overcast, grey and entirely dismal Monday afternoon; weak, insipid light cast it's tendrils around the dull terraced houses. A usually gray town made all the more dull and lifeless by the sheer absence colour, shades of grey. A figure injected some animation into the lifeless scene, a small boy meandering through the puddles that etched the way to his home. Home, that is, in the loosest sense. The boy saw a pile of leaves, stacked at the side of the road, remnants of a summer, a life gone by, the corner of his mouth twitched in an upward direction, a weak smile. It was too much to resist, he ran over and kicked them, in a manner that expressed more anger than one might assume of a small boy indulging in innocent play. A shower of muted reds and gold's erupted around him, a heavy deluge to add to the mist that was insidiously drenching all that it touched. After a few minutes of scattering the neatly swept pile into chaos, he resumed his journey. Stamping in puddles where possible, kicking the odd can or stone, any object that would create an amusing distraction. He was clearly a child who was in no rush to return home.

To look at him he was ordinary, around twelve years old, dark hair, a smattering of freckles across a face that spelled mischief. He was average in build, clothes a little shabby but not quite dishevelled; wearing a school satchel across his shoulders that had seen better days. An observant onlooker might have thought he was a younger sibling, adorning hand me down clothes that had perhaps fit a stockier frame. A child of a working class family. But ordinary, not remarkable, a boy such as a thousand others. Until one looked into his eyes. As deep and dark chocolaty brown as they were, they had no life. A cynicism and hardness emanated from those eyes that would befit a lifer who had spent many years behind prison walls. Eyes that had bore witness to events that were better unseen. Eyes that belied the boys tender years and innocent demeanour.

He continued on his way, reaching a crossroads, absently looking left and right before crossing the road, stoic shoulders hunched against the oppressive atmosphere.

He left the street adorned with a dozen or so barren trees that would erupt into life come spring and then started to make his way into a maze of red brick dwellings. He passed a house with a neat little front garden, a variety of shrubs trimmed within an inch of their lives, a white gravel path leading up to the front door gleamed like marble, the damp air of the cold afternoon leaving jewel like condensation droplets that absorbed any available light. Orange illumination glowed behind the dazzling white of neatly hung net curtains. The house looked inviting to the boy, warm and homely. The house exuded warmth and friendliness, whom so ever crossed the threshold would receive nurturance, love. He glanced sideways at the house, trying not to look but somehow drawn. He whipped his head forward and a flash of anger spread across his face, angered by his weakness or was it longing? It was hard to tell, the look had disappeared as soon as it arrived. He carried on resolutely, head down, hunched shoulders, an attempt to shun the world around him. His gait began to slow and his eyes fixed on a house around three doors down the street. The abode was as unremarkable as the boy. The red brick house gave way to a similarly small red brick wall, which enveloped a slightly shabby lawn. The path leading up to the paint chipped front door had many cracks with weeds breaking to the surface. As the boy approached the house, his gaze rose to the upstairs windows. There were no lights welcoming visitors in from the cold, no signs of life. Threadbare, dull grey curtains framed the windows of the upstairs bedroom like the hair of an old man, peering down on pedestrians passing by. The boy walked slowly up to the house, pausing for the briefest of moments before puffing out his chest in an almost comical manner and slowly opening the door.

With the door closing softly behind him the boy held his breath for a few seconds, cocking his head from side to side, listening intently to the secrets the house might afford him.

Hearing nothing but the ticking of the old clock, shaped like an iconic smiling sun, he slowly let out a breath. Small chest deflating somewhat as he forced himself from the small grey hallway to the right and into the living room. He opened the door and faltered, taking in the scene before him. This was a scene he had witnessed many times; there was no shock or confusion, simply disdain wrapped in sad inevitability. This young boy already knew his fate well, the path he was to lead and the journey he would make, the inevitability of which exposed in one or two faltering steps.

If an angel were to leave the bosom of heaven and gather this boy into his arms, take him away to a place of safety and security, would it change this boy's journey? Would it alter his life to a degree where happiness would become a possibility? There are no angels and this boy did not have the luxury of belief in guardians, angelic or otherwise. He formed a smile by turning up the corners of his mouth; the remainder of his face remained the same, a fixed, cold stare. Surveying the scene before him his solemn eyes scanned from left to right. The room was painted in a dark orange hue, with fashionable large print flower wallpaper to the main wall. Teak veneered furniture adorned the room; a TV was the centrepiece of the room. No cosy open fire, simply a box that sucked in souls and spat out endless trivialities. The television was on, scenes of a mundane nature, a mime extolling the virtues of the best set of chef's knives money could buy. The mime threw a tomato in the air and held a knife out underneath it as if to catch it and the tomato was sliced in half perfectly. The television was muted which made the scene appear surreal, magical. A mediaeval magus brandishing his staff, a weapon of infinite destruction. The flickering of the images spilled into the room, providing the only light save for a table lamp in the corner of the room. The simple, ceramic lamp adorned a small table that displayed pictures of two children. Smiling faces and school uniforms, in various stages of growth. There was a similarity in the faces that suggested family and one of these was the young boy. A coffee table in the centre of the room told the story that had caused the boy's demeanour to change. On the table was a small mirror, traces of white powder doubled in their own reflection; next to this was a piece of clothing. The boy identified the clothing as his mother's, a pink tee shirt with the words "lazy cow" portrayed in a semi-circle beneath a stylized, smiling bovine. The tee shirt was ripped and had streaks of red, sticky viscous fluid that had dripped onto the glossy coffee table. On the floor beside the table was a broken glass, the contents of which had made small rivulets that disappeared underneath the tan leather sofa. The boy's eyes studied the mess in an otherwise neat scene; his eyes followed the traces of the former contents of the glass and caught up with a trail that ran in front of the sofa and towards where he was standing. He turned around slowly and saw the trail leading to the bottom of the stairs. He was snapped from his trance like gaze to the sound of movement upstairs, a door opened and then slammed, footsteps coming down the stairs, heavy and irregular, a stumble against the wall, closer.

* * *

The figure appeared. He was a large man, not exactly overweight but not entirely lean. There was the threat of power beneath the soft fleshiness of his frame. The boy met his eyes, forced smile transforming, becoming genuine. "Johnny!" The man appeared pleased to see the boy "Where've you been, I was expecting you home an hour ago?" The man's voice had the lilt of a small Yorkshire town. The boy did not reply. The man seemed unperturbed by this "Do yer dad a favour and get us another can, bring it upstairs will yer, I've got somert I wanna show yer". With this the man winked at the boy and ruffled his head. A familiar, loving gesture. The boy nodded his head and headed towards the kitchen. Into the kitchen and out of sight of his father the boy began to shake, his trembling hand reached for the fridge door and came into his line of sight. The boy cocked his head at the sight of his hand like an inquisitive puppy. He pulled his it away from the door and forced himself to quiet. The determination on the boy's face resembled that of a child gathering the resolve to win the obstacle race at a schools sports day. After a few seconds, the boy examined his hand, raising it in front of his eyes. Satisfied that he was no longer exhibiting any outward emotion he reached in the fridge and grabbed a four pack of beers. He retraced his steps and ascended the stairs, the gloomy light leaching in through the front door window beginning to fade, following in the footsteps of his father.

Chapter Two

Anna sat at her desk in the noisy, overcrowded office. The buzz of shrill, ringing telephones, some muted and some not so muted conversations, the occasional laugh that resembled a hyena going in for the kill was contributing to the mother of all headaches. To make it worse, it was only half past ten in the morning. She had promised herself a paperwork day. A hectic couple of weeks at work had not earned her any accolades with her managers, rather their wrath for not keeping her paperwork up to date. She had promised faithfully that by the end of the day everything would be in order. All she asked was for one day to tackle the ominous mountain that now lay before her. She surveyed her desk; she assumed it was a desk. In her eyes it appeared to be a floating rectangle of unfinished reports, record sheets, assessments that were due three weeks ago. There was little evidence of anything that remotely resembled wood. She recounted the conversation that had occurred yesterday with her dictator of a manager. Her argument, which in her opinion was completely valid, was met with the scorn and disdain of a woman who had not had sex in a long time, if ever. Anna painted a mental picture of her manager actually indulging in the sex act and decided it was probably best. With a visible shudder Anna picked up a random piece of paper from the floating stock pile. She glanced at it absently, toying with the idea of making a coffee before she started. A caffeine fix would surely be the best course of action? Her phone rang – she feigned annoyance for the benefit of her lurking manager, she was glad of the distraction. "Anna Black, can I help?" a crisp but feminine voice, a twang of Yorkshire with a range of influences, Anna had travelled around since leaving University and her accent all but disappeared. "Mrs Clayton would like to speak with you Anna, she's not very happy..." The receptionist's voice managed to convey the smirk that was placed firmly upon her lips. "Is she ever happy Carly? Unlike yourself, my little ray of sunshine in an otherwise eternal night." "Are you gonna speak to her or not?" Carly's smirk quickly faded, and the clipped telephone voice cracked into the harsh, broad tones of her Batley upbringing. "Do I have a choice?" Before Anna had finished her sentence she heard the click of the line being transferred. "Mrs Clayton, what can I…?" Cut off mid-sentence for the second time in an hour and a half way into her working day Anna pulled the phone handset away from her head. A crackling, screeching noise emanating from it that was audible to all sat within a ten foot radius. Anna tentatively inched the phone closer to her ear. "You fucking bitch! I thought you were supposed to be helping me! I'll break your fucking neck before I let you take my kid!" Anna allowed this to continue for a few minutes. Mrs Clayton was one of a curious breed that was simultaneously able to seriously neglect her child in the pursuit of alcohol and drugs and then blame others for wanting to protect them. No doubt she would soon refer to her darling or her angel through a tearful veil of incongruence. "Mrs Clayton, can I stop you for a second", the shrill cacophony had subdued to the expected sobbing which gave Anna an opportunity to interject. "I take it you have received the papers?" Without giving Mrs Clayton an opportunity to respond Anna continued. "I'm afraid that we have come to the end of the line. Look, I appreciate how upsetting this must be for you, but we have nowhere left to go. You haven't attended the parenting class, you didn't take Whitney for her check-ups, you haven't attended any of the meetings, you won't let me in when I come around to your house, and you are still seeing Dave who is on the register as you know. I'm sorry, Whitney is going to have to become the responsibility of the Local Authority." Anna wasn't sorry. She had seen Whitney on several occasions, a frail little seven year old, curly blond hair and large, heartbreakingly sad brown eyes. It was difficult to talk to the girl, each word seemed to slap her across her face. The anxiety was palpable and this was not the normal state of a seven year old child. Her life should have been filled with laughter and curiosity. Mrs Clayton had ensured that this was not the case. Anna was now debating whether or not a peaceful handover was likely or whether or not she should involve the police. Either way she needed to act quickly. Mrs Clayton was an unpredictable and malicious woman who was as likely to elope with Whitney as she was to waiting at home for Anna and her entourage to arrive, regaling sob stories of her own misfortune. Anna capitalised on the break in the anger at the other end of the line. "Mrs Clayton, I'm going to come over to the house in the next couple of hours, we have a really nice foster family that can care for Whitney until we have sorted out some of these issues. It will give you a break, a chance to recharge and take stock of things and we can take it from there, okay?" A little theatrical sobbing from the recipient of the phone call "Okay, what time will you be here?" "What about twelve noon?" "Okay" Phone slammed down.

Anna walked across the open plan office, a couple of colleagues glanced at her with a "same shit different day" look on their face. She half-smiled back, a typical day in the life of a social worker she mused. Drama, drama, and then a little bit more drama thrown in for good measure. Since starting her career in social work Anna had come to believe that the qualifications were a degree in social work and a masters in masochism. Why else would anyone want to subject themselves to abusive parents, relentless managers and a cruel media on an almost daily basis? "Charlie, I need you to come out on a visit with me, what's your diary like for the next couple of hours?" Charlie looked up from his own impressive mountain of paperwork. Unlike Anna's, Charlie's desk had some semblance of order. Three neat piles, in, out and ongoing Anna surmised. "Anna…" Charlie began one of his get out of jail free speeches. "I have three court reports, two care orders and God knows how many section 17 assessments to finish, Jean has been on my back all week, I really need some paperwork time to…" "Come on Charlie, this is cut and dried, two hours tops, I promise. I'll owe you one?" Anna used all of her persuasive charm. She needed to get on top of this case. Mrs Clayton was turning it up a notch and Anna was concerned that if she didn't get there in the next half hour she would bolt to one of the crack houses she frequented. This may be a burning issue for Anna, but for Charlie and the other workers in this call centre excuse of an office it was the daily routine. "What about lunch, on me, on the way back?" Anna was getting desperate, lunch wasn't an option, a reserve of those fortunate types with "normal" jobs. Jobs that had a beginning, middle and an end each day, with the luxury of breaks and dinner that consisted of something more than a bag of crisps and a coffee glued to a PC screen. She attempted the ruse none the less, desperate times called for desperate measures. She saw her desperation reflected in Charlie's eyes. "Okay, but this better be two hours, or less" Charlie relented with an audible sigh and a slackening on his shoulders. "I promise you, seriously, the foster carers are set up, it's a case of picking up the child, calming down mum, and we will be out of there. You can take mum Charlie, you have a way with the ladies." Anna winked and Charlie grimaced.

* * *

Charlie was still relatively new to the field of social work. He had been mentored by Anna amongst others and felt a loyalty towards his colleagues that would soon be knocked out of him. Charlie had an optimistic approach that he prided himself on. He didn't feel jaded, ground down or sufficiently complained about and this lent itself to a self-assuredness that can only be found in the uninitiated. He was acutely aware of this, and realised that it was only a matter of time before he succumbed to reality. He had great respect for Anna but felt that her disdain with certain cases didn't fully allow her to support them as he saw fit. He also had something to prove, he believed that his worth within the office was tested. Scenarios and case discussions within team meetings gave rise to his radical and progressive musings, fresh from the university lecture halls. Charlie's contributions were met by emotions ranging from amusement to sheer hostility. If Charlie had a pound every time he heard "Well, I've worked in this field for 20 years and I can tell you, people never change!" Charlie wondered if those that proffered this information saw the irony in the statement. Ways of working, new approaches and therapies were constantly being introduced and should be embraced by those working in the field. Charlie was hopeful that as the dinosaurs died out their outdated ideas around child protection would die out with them. However, not all workers in the team were as jaded in their approach. Some welcomed the vitality that a newly qualified worker could bring. Anna and other staff encouraged Charlie to bring forward his ideas, she particularly enjoyed a challenge and liked to debate the theory on what made individuals do what they do. He would eventually gain the respect of the team, he realised that, but would need to clock up a few brownie points over the coming months to speed up the process, he didn't relish being the newbie. It wasn't all bad, his learning curve since joining the team had rocketed and his confidence grew with every day he came to work, his manager gave him more and more difficult, complex cases to work and colleagues were now asking for his assistance, and expertise, with their cases. His positivity and ability to look at the benefits of any given situation had thwarted any thoughts of self doubt. Now, Anna's case, this should be interesting. He closed down his PC, shuffled papers into neat piles on his desk and prepared to leave.

* * *

The flickering light from the PC screen threw elongated, distorted shadows against the walls. A figure of a man, head down, busily navigating the pointer on screen, directing it to do his bidding, complete his work. The images on the screen are cut, spliced, edited. Occasionally, the man sits back in his chair, contemplating, rubbing his chin with deep contemplation, an idea forms and more industry ensues. A particular scene ends and with a few deft clicks of the mouse a red background now appears, words are typed in a rather childish large font, bold, comic sans MS, introducing the next scene, titillating the viewer with what they are about to feast their eyes upon. A slow fade out then leads to more images. A collage of video and stills, a clumsy attempt at direction, but one with which the man applies with seriousness and the utmost dedication. His labours take some time, so concerned is he that the scenes on the pc depict the story he is painstakingly trying to tell. Finally, satisfied with the imagery, he adds sound to the piece, the silent screen suddenly bursts into a cacophony of childish screams and a deep male battle cry. He isn't sure, again leaning back into his chair he contemplates for minutes, allowing the sounds to wash over him. He hangs on every word that is uttered by the players in his film, pondering on their appropriateness to the mood he is attempting to create. He considers, not for the first time, how much easier it would be to insist on a script. Unfortunately, his films were not the kind that would foster the usual rehearsal process. He accepts that he has to work with what he has and appreciates the artistic licence the improvisation afforded him. He clicks his mouse to return the video to it's starting point, having managed to reduce the running time from almost five hours to a more acceptable ninety minutes he ponders which soundtrack to begin with. He had a music file with a "stock" of music he likes to use in his films. The music ranges from The Beatles to Nine Inch Nails, Jimi Hendrix to Killswitch Engage. He liked to have a range of emotional music to draw from. To set the scene, start the watcher of the film on a sentimental journey and finish in bedlam. He chooses "A Perfect Day" by Lou Reed to start the show, the images appeared to fit, he eradicates the sounds from the film itself and overlays with the music. This will be another long process, interjecting his soundtrack with dialogue from his performers, mixing the two when he feels it adds to the piece. Hours later and daylight creeping through his windows he feels he has finished. He had created yet another masterpiece. He reviews the film in it's entirety, knowing that he will have to sleep before reaping the visceral benefits, he is tired, but there are tasks yet to be completed. He inserts a DVD into his PC and hits the burn button. The PC whirs into life, recording the fruits of his labour. He tracks back on the film he has created, an image that will generate much interest, he installed a grossly blown up still on the back of an exciting action shot. The image, a small girl, around seven or eight, she is looking off camera at the leading man, a portion of his elbow had come into view, her eyes wide, a beautifully formed tear in the corner of her left eye on the brink of spilling, an iconic eruption onto an innocent, plump, rosy cheek. The image captured all that he strived for in his artistic endeavours, the loss of innocence.

The man completed his grotesque piece of "art" and ejected a single DVD from his pc. Using a Sharpie to form a moniker on the disc he decided on "Lady and the Tramp", an innocuous title that conveyed, he believed the altogether different content.

He picked up his keys and left the flat, taking with him the DVD, This was part of his ritual. The very first copy need to be treasured, to be hidden away, somewhere safe, an anthology of his work, to be discovered at a later date. Some would be disgusted at the find, others, he believed would be grateful, he was no longer surprised by the connoisseurs of his work, some included those in positions of authority, men of status. He was pleased by this, believed it provided him with a modicum of security. It was also lucrative; he was old school, not like these east European boys, attempting to make a wholesale business, increasing the risk of getting caught. He was discrete, a loner, a connoisseur, he actually enjoyed his work, the cash was a bonus. Following a fifteen minute walk he crossed the main Manchester Road, a long straight road that connected the opposite sides of the Pennines. It wasn't quite dawn and there was no one around, he could hear an odd car engine but in the distance, the area he was in was deserted. He then took a small, narrow side road that secreted a self storage facility. He walked along the length of outdoor lock ups and came across his own. He didn't need a key; a combination lock prevented anyone from entering. Keying in the numbers he then opened the shutter with a great clatter in the early dawn silence. He allowed the sound to evaporate in his ears, cocked head to detect any other movements, nothing. He entered the lock up and switched on the light, drawing down the shutter behind, attempting to make a little less noise. Surveying the space, a three metre by two metre box he calculated that all was in its place. The room was mostly cluttered with junk, old clothes, a Christmas tree, a stack of prints, the foremost being Monet's Sunset. A banal collection of junk. He walked to the back of the room and after some reorganisation of bric a brac uncovered a safe, an old fashioned grey box, again, with a combination lock. Once opened he looked inside, transfixed on the contents. A dozen or more DVD cases, twice as many VHS cassettes filled the safe. He trailed a hand across the fronts of the boxes, nails clicking on every ridge, a shudder escaping the large frame with every scrape of the nail, a sigh, long and low. He took the new edition from his pocket and placed it, reverently with the others. He kissed his fingertips and placed them onto the stack of DVD's as one would place a kiss on a loved one. Retracing his steps he ensured the lock up was secure and ventured into the emerging day.

Chapter Three

Anna and Charlie arrived at Newbold flats, the auspicious dwellings of paedophiles on parole, hard to place individuals with a string of ASBOs and a handful of people working hard to make a living out of the system. All in all a salubrious bunch, not particularly happy to see "officials" turning up on their territory, they were able to talk the talk, mimic a limp when necessary and then return to their homes, smug with the knowledge that they were beating the system, fooling officials. They weren't fooling anyone; it was simply a case of choosing battles wisely. As Anna and Charlie made their way up the graffiti adorned stairwell the stench of urine was almost overpowering. Charlie coughed and covered his mouth with a fist. They passed a young man as they turned to ascend another flight. He was aged between fifteen and twenty five, it was hard to tell, the dark shadows beneath his eyes and snap back hat covering a portion of his face at once reflecting anonymity and likened him to a hundred other youths on this estate alone. As the young man saw them his swagger increased, his gait almost apelike, on each step bending his knee in an exaggerated dance of bravado. He glared at them from under the brim of his hat, looking Anna up and down and sucking air over his teeth. "Hiya" Anna pleasantly greeted the youth before moving past him to ascend the stairs. It was an attempt to disarm him and it worked, a slightly surprised youth continued on his journey and Anna and Charlie made it to the second floor.

Anna turned to Charlie. "Okay, Mrs Clayton knows why we are here, she gave me a bit of a hard time on the phone, but she knows the score. She's already had three kids taken in to care; God knows how she managed to keep hold of Whitney. Anyway, you support her and I'll sort Whitney out, okay?" Charlie shrugged his shoulders, a sign of acquiescence. Charlie had not met Mrs Clayton but he was sure that she could change the path she was walking through her life, and ultimately protect Whitney's. At once he admired Anna for the stoic way she handled these situations, emotionless and with an ultimate goal in mind. The safety of the child to Anna was black and white. Get the child away from this situation and the rest, the child's life, ideology, hopes and dreams would be met by some transient strangers, the foster carers. But what about the lives they were about to tear apart? Mrs Clayton had most likely suffered her own demons, how could she, without guidance and support be able to offer her offspring the nurturing environment that she had never experienced? Charlie believed in the infinite good, in that all humans were capable of change, all Mrs Clayton needed was a catalyst for this and perhaps he was the one to provide it? As experienced and knowledgeable as Anna was, she had that air of cynicism about her that in Charlie's opinion, did not belong in social work. Charlie's musings did not go unnoticed. "Are you okay Charlie, you look a little annoyed, have I said something to piss you off?" Anna asked in a manner that indicated she was reading his mind. Charlie straightened up, "No, no, I'm fine. Right so I'll sort out mum, you sort out Whitney. Come on then, I haven't got all day." Charlie grinned, a not so convincing grin and shuffled his feet; he didn't like this level of self-exposure. Anna had a way of bringing out both the best and the worst of him, and this made him uncomfortable.

* * *

Anna knocked on the door. It was painted red, the same colour as every other door on this floor. No individuality save for the battering the door had clearly suffered, paint chipped away and ugly smears of what one hoped was earth from an angry shoe. The door flew open and an extremely irate Mrs Clayton suddenly replaced the miserable red door. "Yer fucking 'ere are yer! Come to take my fucking kid yer bastard! An' who's he? Yer fucking body guard?" She was expecting this kind of tirade, it was par for the course, briefly wondering if she should have involved the police Anna replied "No, he isn't, can we come inside Mrs. Clayton, you don't want the neighbors to hear your private business do you?" Anna's voice was calm and reassuring. As she spoke, she edged towards the doorway, Mrs. Clayton instinctively moving aside to let her through. Anna continued, "Mrs. Clayton, you know why we are here, I know it's hard for you. We just want what's best for Whitney and I know that you do too." "Course I want what's best for her, she's my kid, and what's best for her is to stay wi' er mum." Anna had managed to sidle into the hallway during the exchange; she glanced at Charlie with an urgent look in her eye, encouraging him to do the same. If they didn't gain access to the house, the police would then definitely need to back them up and the whole drama would end up being much more traumatic than the situation called for. "Mrs. Clayton, may I introduce myself?" Mrs. Clayton appeared bemused by this rather formal request; a smirk began to spread across her face. Charlie took in the form of Mrs. Clayton. She was a rather large woman, in stature as well as girth. She sported the typical garb of the local residents, dark blue tracksuit bottoms that had seen better days, and an ill-fitting tee shirt, grey marl and leaving no one under the illusion that she could do with losing a few pounds. Her hair was a dirty blonde, scraped back into a ponytail so tight that it possibly reduced her visible age by ten years. Charlie at once felt pity for this human stood before him, a product of her environment, she would once have had such potential. He imagined, as he always did of his most challenging clients, a newborn baby, fresh from the womb, a blank slate that could be written upon with nurturing, positive and loving pastels or scrawled upon in thick, greasy, indelible marker. It was a random world that each new born found itself in, and would have to adapt to, he felt a wave of pity. He smiled at her, a twinkle in his grey, blue eyes and a warm face that caught her off guard. She regarded him curiously, he wasn't quite sure if she viewed him as something to be toyed with or saw in him the empathy that he was desperately trying to find. "Go on then, who are you?" "Thank you Mrs. Clayto…" She stopped him "Julie, that's me name, there's no point being so fucking formal given what yer doin'" Charlie knew he had half won the battle. Julie's tone of voice had decreased in decibels and pitch, she was warming to him. "Julie, could we go into the living room for a chat, would that be ok with you?" "Yea, come in." Julie responded with a degree of bravado but clearly less agitated than she had been when answering the door. Julie led Charlie and Anna into a sparsely furnished room. A worn beige sofa spanned the length of one wall; a large LCD TV adorned the opposite wall and a small coffee table between the two. The table had a crumpled TV magazine and several coffee stains that could only have developed their intense colour with age, nothing else. The floor, a light beech laminate bore similar battle scars. Julie flopped down onto the sofa, the impact of her weight causing the cushions either side of her to bounce, as if in attempt to flee. Charlie motioned a hand towards the other end of the sofa, quietly relieved it was particularly large. Julie nodded and indicated that he be seated. Anna stood in front of them both "Mrs. Clayton, I need to see Whitney, explain to her what's going on?" Julie glanced at Anna, it appeared that she had forgotten she was in the room, or the equation at all. She turned her gaze back to Charlie "Yea, she's in 'er room, you know where it is, you've checked it out often enough." A sarcastic snigger escaped her lips.

* * *

Anna quietly left the room confident that Charlie was winning Mrs Clayton over. She wanted the removal of Whitney to be as calm and incident free as possible. Anna made her way down the hall to Whitney's bedroom. She knocked gently on the door "Whitney? It's Anna." No response, Anna placed her hand on the door handle and inched the door open calling Whitney's name as she did so. The last thing she wanted was to scare the child, she had been through enough. Anna poked her head around the door and saw Whitney sat on her bed; she was playing with a bedraggled, old doll. The doll was the kind that imitated a new born baby, it was naked and had biro marks upon its body akin to home made tattoos. Whitney was a beautiful child, as all children are. She was slight in stature, perhaps more so than other well nourished children her age, with delicate features, a mop of blond curly hair and large brown eyes. Whitney's eyes reminded Anna of those depicted in Japanese cartoons. Unrealistically large, exceptionally beautiful and always threatening a tear. Whitney looked up at Anna from her bed with little surprise. She continued to bounce the doll on her lap. The room was grim, a litter of clothing, dirty plates with upturned forks waiting to enter an unwary foot. The walls were covered in graffiti that the previous occupant had clearly enjoyed scrawling given the numerous exclamation marks following expletives. There were no curtains to cover the small window that was lined with a black scum. Despite the many efforts to provide Mrs Clayton with funds and vouchers to decorate the room it had never happened. The single bed was the only concession she had made to ensure her daughter's comfort.

"I don't like that man" Whitney stated, without any emotion other than slight annoyance. Anna slowly walked up to Whitney's bed and gently sat down next to her. "Which man?" Anna asked softly, brushing a stray lock of hair from Whitney's face. "That man, he's horrible and I don't like him" With this Whitney folded her arms indignantly and turned over on the bed to faced away from Anna.

The hairs that prickled on the back of Anna's neck turned an otherwise comical gesture into something more sinister. The haunted look in the little girl's eyes indicated this statement needed some exploration. That would have to wait; right now she needed to get Whitney into a place of safety. Anna had had serious concerns regarding the company that Mrs Clayton liked to keep and knew that Whitney's safety was at risk. However, despite her concerns no solid evidence had come to light that Whitney had been subject to anything but the cruel neglect of her mother. With only a gut feeling and no evidence to back it up Anna had not been able to involve the police. It had taken what seemed like years to get the approval of her manager and the "panel" to move the case into proceedings at all. It would seem that these days a worker needed video evidence of abuse before they were able to speak to a parent, let alone protect a child.

"Whitney, I need to talk to you sweetie." Anna stood up and moved to the other side of the bed so that Whitney could see her face. "Your mum isn't feeling so good at the moment. We all think it would be a good idea if you spent some time with another family until she is feeling a bit better. Is that OK Whitney?" No response, Whitney looked straight past Anna and into her own thoughts. "I'm going to get some of your clothes together Whitney, is there anything you would like to take with you?" Whitney sat up on the bed, seeming to snap out of a daydream, "Where am I going?" Her voice was barely more than a whisper, so fragile her words seemed to disappear on her lips like a wisp of smoke. "You're going to stay with a nice family; they have a daughter about your age so you'll be able to play with her." Anna attempted to sound upbeat about the prospect of Whitney being snatched from her mother, the only woman, good or bad that she had identified with and loved. "Can I still see mum?" "Of course you can sweetie, we'll arrange for you to see mum as often as we can" Anna wasn't sure but she felt she saw disappointment in the child's eyes. That was unusual, Anna had been in many situations where horrifically abused children were devastated at the separation with their parents, regardless of the pain inflicted, children remained loyal to their parents. There were usually tears, resistance and trauma. Anna wondered whether the disappointment that registered in Whitney's face was because she was being separated from her mum, or whether she would have to visit with her. "OK Whitney, come and help me pack, what would you like to take?" Anna wanted to move quickly, the ill feelings she had had whilst working this case were intensifying and she felt an impulsive need to get this child out of the house. Whitney climbed off her bed and walked up to Anna, still clutching her doll. They proceeded to pack a bag.

Chapter Four

Charlie smiled at Julie "You love Whitney don't you?" he stated this in a simple, matter of fact tone but conveyed with it a kindness and forgiveness that would allow her to open up to him. "'Course I do, what a stupid thing to say. She's all I 'av is Whitney. That pig 'as fucked me off. He said he's got another bird. I did everything for 'im an' all," Julie's intense stare fell towards her feet, she became quieter and seemed surprisingly genuine in the sadness she now displayed. "Who are we talking about Julie?" Charlie's voice had changed pitch to match hers; he spoke quietly, gently, coaxing her. "My fella, I know you lot said he was on the register but he wasn't a fucking pedo, he took the blame for his brother. He loved my Whitney and she loved 'im, he was always playing with 'er, and not in a fucking weird way if that's what yer thinking" "How long were you together Julie?" "I dunno, about six months, but I knew 'im before that. He knows mi brother, the've bin mates for ages. He used to come round t'house wi our Kev." She referred to her brother Kevin West, another soul that had passed through social services doors on a path to a life of crime. Kevin had a learning disability and could be easily manipulated. He was targeted for sport by peers as a youth and nothing much had changed apart from his tormentor's techniques. Now he regarded them as friends. Julie straightened up, suddenly unsure of herself, Charlie had the feeling that she had said more than she had planned to. He was aware that Anna would be with the child attempting to organise her for the removal. "We'll need to organise contacts with Whitney Julie, which days would be best for you?" Julie looked at Charlie blankly, almost appearing to stare right through him. "Julie, you do know what's happening don't you?" Julie sighed and with it gathered herself up from the sofa, appearing much larger than she had a moment ago. "Yea, I know, your taking my fucking kid off me." As Julie turned towards the doorway Anna appeared with a fragile looking Whitney behind her. "Would you like to say goodbye to Mum, Whitney?" Anna turned to the child who simply starred at her mother, making no attempt to move towards her. "OK Mrs Clayton, we'll give you a call tomorrow to sort out contact arrangements and I'll be able to let you know how Whitney has settled, is that okay?" Julie ignored Anna completely, she moved surprisingly quickly given her generous girth towards the child. Whitney took a very small step back and then appeared to steel herself against her mother's approach. Julie bent down and gathered Whitney into her arms, Julie whispered something inaudible to her daughter and then hugged her in what appeared to be an almost painful grasp. Anna intervened, she slipped her hand into Whitney's "OK kiddo, lets go. Mrs Clayton, I'll be in touch tomorrow" Anna headed for the door, the anxiety she had felt previously rising in her again, she focused on not breaking into a run and huddled Whitney through the door and down along the walkway to the stairs. Charlie lingered for a moment. "Are you Ok Julie?" he asked. "Do I look OK?" Charlie actually felt that she did, he could not imagine a situation where he would be forcibly parted from a child, his child. It seemed unfathomable. But Charlie's life was a far cry from her own. He had a perfectly normal upbringing, loving parents, guitar lessons, birthday parties and help with homework. Julie on the other hand had been lucky to survive. He didn't know the details of the case but through general lunchtime discussions with Anna he knew that Julie had been through the mill. "There but for the grace..." he muttered under his breath as he made his way to the door. He looked back and regarded Julie, she was stood with her back against the hall wall, facing him but head directed to her hand. Her thumbs frantically conveying some message to some person via her mobile phone. "Goodbye Julie" Charlie said gently, she didn't look up; her message was obviously far too consuming to be interrupted by pleasantries. Charlie closed the door quietly behind him as he exited the miserable flat.

Chapter Five

After what seemed like an age they pulled up to a neat and tidy red bricked house on a tree lined street on the outskirts of the town, suburbia in a word. All wheelie bins were tucked out of sight, lawns mown within an inch of their lives, a variety of potted plants were so uniform in their designation that one had the impression that they were thrown in with each house sale. A "nice" street, Anna mused, "safe". The area that they had arrived at, Shelley was a curious mix of old stone terraced houses and new build estates, a very good school, little bistros and coffee shops. An affluent and up and coming area where housing was still affordable, if a tiny stone terrace was to your liking, of course. The trip from Julie's flat to their destination should have taken perhaps 20 minutes, thirty at the most. Whitney however had prolonged the journey by insisting on three toilet breaks. Anna was aware that the girl must be nervous, and wanted to attribute the errant bladder on this reason. However, Whitney appeared calm, blunted, as if sedated and a gnawing thought was scratching away at Anna's sub conscience. "Right, Charlie, I'll take Whitney into the foster carers and get her settled and then take you back to the office, OK?" "Not a problem Anna, would you like me to come in?" "Its fine, give me twenty minutes, Whitney, come on hun, let's go inside, they're expecting us." Anna took the little girl's hand and led her along the driveway and side of the house to a neat porch. They walked slowly, she did not want to rush her, Anna gave some comforting words to the doll like girl, a waif in the truest sense. She was brave, her step, whilst slow and deliberate, didn't falter, she kept Anna's pace. A pang of sadness hit Anna hard. She pushed the associated thoughts to the back of her mind, the whys and hows, Whitney, along with many others, was so vulnerable, Anna was constantly astounded by the suffering adults could inflict on their infant offspring. She pressed the doorbell, looking down and winking at the stoic child, Whitney returned a weak smile.

The door was opened with a flurry of warmth and activity. "Ah, you must be Whitney" Gail beamed at her. "Come on inside darling" Gail proceeded to make a fuss of her for the next five minutes, her own daughter looking on with a pleasant smile, husband tending to her bag. Anna interjected, "Why don't you take Whitney upstairs and show her the room?" She addressed Gail's daughter. Gail, sensing that Anna needed to speak with her agreed. "Yes, take Whitney to see her room and then maybe to see the rabbits in the garden. Do you like rabbits Whitney?" She nodded a slightly nervous nod. Big eyes looked at Anna, trying to read some confirmation that this was all Ok. "Go on Whitney. I'll come and see you before I go."

When the girls had disappeared from view, Gail turned to Anna "Is everything alright?" A concerned look was creasing the usually wrinkle free skin on her face. "Yes, well as alright as it can be given the circumstances. One thing and it's probably nothing. She needed to pee three times on the way here. I appreciate she might be nervous but can you keep an eye on things. Check her out when she has a bath later, let me know if there are any concerns. I'm going to have her examined by the paediatrician anyway, but…" she trailed off, unable to put her finger on the concerns she had, was it something in the child's eyes? A need to pee was typical in a case like this. The girl was scared, she'd just been taken away from her mother, placed with strangers, of course she was going to be nervous. But there was something more, she wondered if the "man" had something to do with it. "I will do," Gail broke her train of thought. "Any issues and I'll give you a call. When is she likely to see the doctor?" "Hopefully tomorrow. I'll let you know. Thanks for taking her Gail, I'm sure she'll be happy here with you guys." Anna said her goodbyes to Whitney who was by now in the garden, gently stroking one of the pet rabbits, a small smile on her face. "I'll see you very soon kiddo,"

It had been a long day, Anna made her way back to the car. She had a few chores left to complete and would then attempt to organise her thoughts. Figure out how to scratch the itch in her head.

Chapter Six

The boy ascended the stairs, each one a slow, yet determined stride into his future. His mind wandered to reflections of the day that had just passed. He pondered school, classmates, algebra, packed lunches, teachers droning, bells ringing, all superfluous, alien mediocrities that did not apply to him. He lived in a very different world, a cruel and bloody world that no one seemed to recognise. He lived two very separate lives. One that had its anchor in normality, of soap operas and school, fall outs with friends, visits to aunts and uncles. The other life was, to him, separate and yet inextricably linked to the former. This world was sordid, cruel, and painful. One transposed over the other. He was a child, unable to reconcile the two extremes, they became blended, parts of the whole, a distorted view of the world at the same time normal and grotesque. He wondered at times why others could not see the atrocities that he witnessed played across his young face, notice the miniscule but guilt ridden specks of blood on his clothing or hear the emotion that caused the hint of a tremor on his lips. But they didn't. The boy realised that even if they did, they wouldn't care, his father had taught him that much, there were no angels, no one could save him. This was his life, he had to comply or face the consequences. The boy was unaware of this fact but he was in the midst of creation, he was being shaped and moulded to become the monster that destiny dictated. The fragments of innocence that remained were being eroded through self-preservation that would transform into desire, lust, a blood lust. A transformation was occurring, at what point this finally took hold and the child that was would be consumed no one would ever know, a lost boy.

The boy heard a moan, it was a guttural, throaty moan, it would have made the hairs on the back of grown men's necks stand on end, but the boy continued, the mouth smile returning to his face, eyes dead. Shuffling sounds emanated from inside his parents' bedroom in addition to a tune that's was emanating from a radio or a CD player. The tune was old, to the boy ancient. A heavy rock tune that his father listened to from time to time. The soft thud of the familiar tune was hypnotic, beckoning the boy inside... He finally ascended the stairs and stood in front of a door. The door was painted white, a plain door, nothing remarkable about it other than a red smear, brown at the edges where the liquid that had caused it was starting to dry. The smear was close to the handle, as if the bearer of the smear had opened the door and left their red brown legacy behind them. "This is where I am" the smear spoke to the boy. He hesitated for the slightest moment, only a trained eye would have noticed the split second of reluctance and then he placed his steady hand on the door knob and opened the door.

The woman lay on the bed, head faced towards the window away from the boy. It was apparent that she was the source of the moaning. She lay in a foetal position, knees drawn up tightly to her chest. She was naked, the only contrast on her pale flesh were splashes of the red brown liquid that had marked her trail to this room. Her face was covered, as were the pillows that her face now lay upon, with blood, some fresh, some dried to a flaky brown consistency. The boy regarded her, her lips mouthed inaudible words that he could not hear nor wanted to know the meaning of. The woman did not look at the boy as he entered the room, she appeared to be elsewhere, in a place where the horrors she were currently being subjected to didn't exist. Along with the blood smeared across her face there were specks of white powder. Mercifully, the woman was narcotically oblivious to the worst of her fate.

The boy looked from the woman to his father, he stood over her like a grizzly bear waiting for the moment he could swipe his killing blow, a grin on his face and glint in his eye. "What took yer? This bitch is waiting for the boys!!" The last word was drawn out, jubilant, akin to a best man on a stag night referring to a lap dance in a strip bar. The boy smiled at the man. He proffered him the alcohol. "Nice one son, Av got a right thirst coming on!" With this he laughed a hateful, menacing laugh. The boy chuckled. He glared at the woman on the bed, disgust and hatred filled the boy's eyes. It was clear he did not view a human being before him, he saw something to revile, a thing not worth his emotions. His emotions, or what hollow empty shadows appeared to be left of them, were reserved for the man stood before him, his father, the man who had created him, taught him what life was really all about. He both loved and feared this man. His father had lavished him with affection with gifts and knowledge. He had also illustrated that his mother was a junkie whore, and that she did not deserve his love or pity. She deserved to be punished. The boy eventually agreed with this perspective, he began to see the weaknesses in his mother that his father alluded to. He would often find her crying, the tell-tale signs of drug use in the house when he returned from school. The half-conscious, half-hearted attempts at a conversation "Hey babe, how's it going my little man?" drifting off into a drug fuelled stupor before he had any time to respond. She wasn't there for him, she was no mother. His father had told him, in great detail, of the men she had slept with, sneaking out while the boy was at school to indulge in illicit affairs. She was a junkie whore, and he hated her. She, as far as the boy was concerned, deserved everything that was coming to her.

* * *

The boy's father walked around to the other side of the bed. Beneath the window which was framed with grey curtains was a dressing table. He pulled a can from the four pack and slammed the remaining three onto the dresser. The noise caused the boy to turn his eyes away from the woman on the bed to where his father stood. His eyes surveyed the dresser, along with the pack of beer there was a hairbrush, the boy could make out the strands of hair that had become entangled with the brush. Long and blonde, his mothers, perhaps his sister's. Alongside the brush were a variety of implements, some that would ordinarily be seen in a workshop or garage. Indicating that some DIY project or other was taking place in the bedroom. This was not the case. The man noticed his son's gaze and looked from the boy to the assortment of tools on the dresser. "She's been at it again son" the man had a mock seriousness in his voice that was almost comedic. "We need to teach 'er a lesson, yeah?" The boy smiled and nodded, a cruel smile. "Yer sister's staying with yer nana, so no interruptions, eh?" the man laughed, seemingly finding this comment amusing. The boy had ascertained that these "punishments" only occurred when his sister wasn't present. She wasn't like him. She didn't know what kind of a monster her mother was; even if she did the boy doubted she would be happy with the justice the boy and his father liked to exact on her. Well more fool her, the boy believed that she would end up just like her mother, a junkie or a whore, or both. He secretly relished the idea of exacting the same punishment on his sister as he did on this pathetic excuse of a human being cowering in front of him right now. He would bide his time. His father seemed to believe that his sister was beyond reproach, but he did not. "Right then son, what'll it be?" His father's hand traced across the tools that were lined up on the dresser. A small sanding device, drill, blowtorch, pliers. "Come on lad, you choose. The boy walked over to his father, eyes fixed to a particular tool "Drill" he stated matter of factly. He picked up the drill; it looked far too large, too cumbersome for the boy to handle. He brandished it like a weapon, reminiscent of the child soldiers in far off, war torn countries. He approached the bed. His mother lay with her eyes closed, blissfully ignorant of the scene that had just played out before her. This peace wouldn't last long. The boy held out the drill and prodded her forehead with the sharp drill bit. The woman stirred, slowly opened her eyes, shrugging off her narcotic haze to take in the reality that was about to unfold around her. Her eyes did not display fear exactly, it was there, but more resignation and sadness as her fate became apparent in the eyes of those that should have loved her.

Chapter Seven

Anna stared at the digital clock in her car, it was already 4:45pm and she still had a million things to do. She had delivered Whitney to the foster family and this had taken significantly longer than anticipated. They were a nice couple, one of the more desirable names on the rogue's gallery list of foster carers the local authority used. Wholesome, Anna contemplated, yes wholesome described them well. They attended church, their daughter, who was just a little older than Whitney had piano lessons and was already on her way to a grade eight, was a clever, articulate and polite child. Anna was relieved that she had finally managed to rescue Whitney, was that the right word, rescue? It was her job and it wasn't a job that was held in particularly high esteem, in fact quite the opposite. "Rescuer of children" was possibly the last thing the people she worked with would ascribe to her. It was the last thing she would ascribe to herself for that matter. Eventually even the most enthusiastic, ideological social workers were ground down under the weight of bureaucracy. The children became "cases", reduced to paperwork to finish off, deadlines. She was surprised that she felt she had rescued the girl; this case must be getting to her. "I just need to make a couple of phone calls Charlie, then I'll drop you at the office, OK?" Charlie looked up from the notes he was scribbling and nodded. Anna felt guilty, she realised that she had taken up much of his day when he had his own cases to deal with, she made a mental note to make it up to him. Anna then proceeded to organise a visit for Whitney to the paediatrician, she then spoke with her manager to give her an update and finally she asked the admin to sign both herself and Charlie out of the office. This was no easy task, it consisted of trying to hold conversations on a cheap, office issue mobile phone. The design of the phone was clearly for text messages only as the reception caused the caller and the called to repeat each sentence at least three times. One could easily become stressed to the point of admission to hospital under a section of the mental health act by using the office equipment alone, let alone the actual case work. "Finally, done!" By now it was 5:10pm. It was a half hour drive back to the office to drop Charlie off and Anna still had to write up the details of the day's events. She would do this at home, following a dinner that would probably consist of canned soup and an out of date yoghurt that might still be lurking at the back of her fridge. She couldn't face stopping off at the supermarket to shop for groceries. It had been a difficult day and she just wanted to get home and contemplate the situation. Try to piece together the information she had and determine if her suspicions were founded. "Do you fancy getting something to eat?" Charlie asked this as if reading her mind. "I was just thinking about dinner Charlie, how strange." "Not strange at all, it's around the time that most people do eat" he responded with a gentle smile. Anna regarded Charlie, his face was non-committal, there was no intent, there didn't appear to be a hidden agenda. That's what she liked about him, what you see is what you get. "Why not, I did promise you lunch. Anyway I could do with bouncing a few ideas around" "Great, there's a Pizza Hut not far from the office, we can eat there and then it won't take me too long to get back to the car". "Mmmm, pizza" Anna's guttural tones paid homage to Homer Simpson. They both smiled.

* * *

"So, what do we know about Dave then?" Anna asked as she pushed an errant cube of beetroot around her plate. The beetroot was all that was left of an all you can eat salad and half, possibly two thirds, of a hot and spicy deep pan. "Hmm, David Cartwright" Charlie was mulling this over whilst finishing his remaining significantly smaller share of the meal. David Cartwright was the person of undesirable character that Mrs Clayton had been having liaisons with, against Social Services advice. "I have heard of him, he caused a bit of a concern in a case I had last year. Similar circumstances, mother was associating with him against our advice but it seemed to be a bit of a flash in the pan romance. She quickly found another beau, not on any kind of register as far as we know. Well the police checks came back clean and he actually seems to be a good influence on the kids." Charlie became lost in his story. It was a success story, mum and kids were now doing really well, with help from her new boyfriend mum had really managed to turn things around. She accepted support from Charlie, was willing to make the changes in her life that would keep her kids safe. Good work can be done. He glanced up at Anna, she was waiting expectantly for him to continue. "Sorry" a quiet chuckle. "I drifted off a minute there. Where we're we, yes David Cartwright. I know that he's a schedule one offender, on the register. He had a bit of a crappy upbringing. Loads of domestic violence call outs, his dad was a real piece of work. His mother eventually abandoned the family and he and his sister were taken into care. There were various interventions, psychology and therapies, his sister seemed to turn out Ok but he ended up with YOT." Charlie referred to the Youth Offending team, they liked to use a "reward" system to encourage young offenders to remain on the straight and narrow. What they didn't realise, and yet everyone else did, was that they only supplemented the ill-gotten gains of the wards in their care. It was a softly, softly approach that didn't seem to work, generally staffed by unrealistic workers that believed in the concept of rehabilitation via monetary reward. Anna had little time for them, Charlie, being the less cynical of the two could relate to their principles but had yet to be completely convinced about effectiveness. But if they managed to get one out of ten kids off the rocky road to the criminal justice system it was better than none. "What do we know about his index offences?" "Well, he was charged with a few assaults on young girls when he was around 19 maybe 20. The M.O was to ingratiate himself with a family and then offer to babysit. The parents would come home to find the child in distress and Dave trying to convince them that the kid had had some kind of nightmare. This happened with a couple of family's but it's highly likely there were more, much of this kind of thing goes unreported. The CPS only brought charges on the two I mentioned and he received a custodial for a few months. Then he seemed to disappear for a while. Until recently of course." Anna mulled this information over, she had gathered some information on this man, but as soon as she hit the fact that he was on the sex offenders register she had focused on Whitney and her mother, letting mum know that Social Services were not happy with her placing her child at risk by associating with a known sex offender. As far as she was concerned he was a threat to the child, the whys and wherefores were superfluous. So it seemed that he was a fucked up youth, so what? There were thousands of them; it didn't mean they had to turn into abusers. At the end of the day, Anna believed we all had our crosses to bear. Each individual has a choice of the path they decide to take, and some proved to turn to the path less travelled. She clearly needed to do some research. Try and find out what, if anything this man had been getting into. He had approached the family Charlie had been working with, perhaps he had approached others?

"OK, enough!" Anna slapped her hands on the table before her and pushed herself back in her seat. "I'm sure it must be close to bed time. Thanks for today Charlie, you really helped me out." Anna smiled sincerely at Charlie, she had genuinely appreciated having him on board today, he handled Mrs Clayton well, he would make an excellent social worker once the green had been washed from behind his ears. "No problem, look it's not quite bedtime, "a grin, was he flirting with her? "I was going to watch a film tonight, a Del Torro I've been wanting to see. You need to switch off for a while. I know you Anna, I bet you have your laptop in the car, you'll be working till God knows what time. Why don't you come back to mine for a couple of hours?" She regarded Charlie, he was a nice guy, appeared genuine, she liked him, but not that in that way. Anna had far too many close calls behind her to appreciate that "platonic" was another meaning for "matter of time". The silence and glance lasted just a little too long, he visibly blushed and shuffled in his seat. "Ok, I'm sorry bad idea, you're right, it's getting late." He looked at his wrist that didn't contain a watch, took his wallet from his pocket and left a note on the table. Anna started to protest but he held up his hand. Not wanting to add to his clear embarrassment she said nothing. "See you tomorrow Anna." He left the restaurant.

* * *

She felt a little guilty, but not too much. He'd get over it. On the drive home she mused over her several failed relationships. On reflection, it was easy to blame her partners for the numerous ways the relationship had ended but she had to take some responsibility herself. She could be a difficult person to live with, she had never felt comfortable enough to reveal all of herself to any of her partners, a romantic chameleon, she made visible to her significant others only the parts of herself that she knew would appeal. This had left her dissatisfied, never knowing what real, complete and all-consuming love was. How could she know, she had never given herself completely, entrusting another with her weaknesses, her secrets, her passions. Although, she determined, her last sad, failed attempt at coupledom she could blame entirely on him. It had taken her a while to figure it out, he was good, she gave him that much credit. At first he lavished her with gifts and trips, knew all of the right things to say, made her feel that this could actually be it, the one and then she discovered his wandering eye. That term had always amused Anna, She envisioned a man deemed to have one with a mollusc like stalk in the middle of his forehead, eye perched neatly atop the stalk, and said eye moving independently from the rest of the head, wandering. The reality of those afflicted with the wandering eye, or more specifically the partners of those afflicted, was not so amusing. She remembered an incident where her ex partner's condition flared up while they were shopping for groceries one Friday evening. The target of the wandering eye was located on the bread and cereal isle. With military precision the target was locked onto, eye ready to launch. Her ex had hung back from Anna, feigning interest in a new flavour of bagel, but the eye gave itself away, whilst attempting to communicate with Anna it could not leave its target for more than a second at a time. Anna had turned to look at the object that was causing the eye to almost leave its stalk, not very surprisingly a young, pretty brunette, completely unaware of the covert military exercise the eye was conducting browsed over muesli. This charade continued throughout the entire shopping experience. This kind of thing happened on a regular basis. It made Anna uncomfortable, angry and in some cases a little embarrassed. Her ex would try to explain away actions with ridiculous excuses and would see nothing wrong with his behaviour at all, his responses usually had an air of indignation, a childlike "why do you have to spoil my fun". It took quite a considerable amount of time but Anna eventually felt that she was having to admonish a child for mischievous behaviour. Anna realised she didn't want to have a relationship with a child, let alone a child that had a rather loathsome affliction, she grew extremely tired of this behaviour, and yet another one bit the dust. She realised Charlie's request for a potential "date" had thrown her off guard, the last thing she wanted at the moment was any kind of relationship. She decided to put it out of her mind, she reiterated to herself that he would get over it and their working relationship would resume.

* * *

Anna owned a small, stone terraced house, typical of the town in which she lived. She loved her home, it was tastefully decorated to reflect the period in which it was built, Anna believed this to be modern Victorian if there was such a style. It was cosy and warm and felt safe and snug, lots of purples, dark reds and greens, akin to a jewel tinted womb. There was one thing she didn't like about her home, however, her fridge. Anna rarely shopped for more than one meal at a time, occasionally two at the weekend. Yet she was constantly disappointed when she opened it to find very little in it, as if expecting the fridge to populate itself with tasty delicacies. As she entered the house, according to ritual, her bag was dumped in the hallway, door locked behind her, she made her way to the kitchen and then the fridge to determine whether just this once, there was actually something edible in it. She wasn't particularly hungry having just dined on fattening pizza and equally fattening salad, but she was a creature of habit. Anna flicked on the kettle switch and returned to the hallway to retrieve her bag. She caught site of herself in a gilt framed mirror that hung at the bottom of a narrow, royal blue carpet cladded staircase. She looked tired, her shoulder length, dark hair was tucked back behind her ears, exposing her face to it's fullest. Her eyes were encircled with dark shadows, the usual glint dulled, her complexion looked pale and her face a little drawn. A frown furrowed her brow, not the most appealing of expressions she contemplated. She needed a break, maybe take a short holiday in the sun, she had plenty of leave owed to her and realised she couldn't remember that last time she had spent a significant amount of time away from the office, barring the odd bank holiday. Anna resolved to book some leave first thing tomorrow. But first things first, she dug out her laptop and decided she needed to conduct a little research into Mr David Cartwright.

Twelve fifteen. It was time for bed. Three mugs of tea and several hours after she had decided to look up David Cartwright on the social services database Anna had learned some uncomfortable facts. It would seem that Dave liked to ingratiate himself with women who might be deemed vulnerable in some way, they also all appeared to have young children, girls.

The scant information from the Social Services records formed a sketchy picture. Following Dave's convictions in his late teens he had disappeared from sight, well, the sight of Social Services at least, there could be criminal convictions that did not involve those on the database she had access to. He then re-emerged several years later in connection with a child protection case in which the sexual abuse of a nine year old girl was suspected but never proved. The child's mother vehemently denied that Dave would do such a thing and blamed her ex-partner, the child's father. From the files, it would appear that both men were questioned about the assaults but it came to nothing. It was a tragic fact that of the known cases of sexual abuse a very small fraction ends up with a conviction, so this was by no means out of the ordinary. Strangely, terrified, traumatised children did not make the best witnesses. He was also associated with two further historical files. The files had been closed due to the families moving out of area. It appeared that in both cases Social Services were unaware of the area that the families had moved to. Workers had turned up for visits and the families, both single parents and mothers of young daughters, had simply moved out. Police had been alerted in both cases, however, there were no further entries in their files thus Anna surmised that they had not been traced. This wasn't particularly unusual in itself. Some families known to social services were transient, they would move from town to town, slipping through the net until some complaint or another was made. In both cases there were ongoing concerns regarding the mothers' ability to care for their children, and in both cases David Cartwright was recorded as mum's partner. Anna shuddered involuntarily. She had a very uneasy feeling about this case, there was something more to it, she didn't want to jump to any conclusion, however, David Cartwright seemed to be a very bad man. She would call the vulnerable victims unit tomorrow and try to get the police involved. With that thought Anna packed away her laptop and retreated upstairs to her bed, forgoing a shower she slipped into the cool sheets. Looking at a photograph on her bedside table, as she always did, a smile crossed her face. The photo was old, it depicted a happy family holiday scene, three heads poked into the round holes of seaside cartoon figures, faces beaming out from the plywood cut-out at strange angles to the ruddy faced characters. Her mother and father glancing down at Anna's laugh. Caught in a moment, fond memories of her childhood. The following year it would be she and her father that visited the seaside town, her mother, months previously having succumbed to a particularly vigorous type of ovarian cancer. They had walked the paths they had walked the previous year, ghosts revisiting old memories, seeking solace in the wonderful time they had been granted, a loving, nurturing mother and her father's soul mate. The experience of losing her mother at a young age had brought two things to Anna's life, the fleeting nature of human existence which had fuelled her desire to live out her life as her mother had, with a love and compassion for all. And the realisation that the bond between herself and her father could never be lost, despite his grief he became Anna's mother and father, her guidance and support. Unlike many of the parents Anna came across during the course of her work, her father had taken his role of parent seriously, attempting to construct a confident and enthusiastic young woman, with a value base that would ensure she would seek her own identity with integrity. She hoped he was proud of her, saying goodnight to the photograph she attempted to sleep.

Chapter Eight

"Poppy! Poppy, stop that, what have you got there girl?" The small West Ireland terrier completely ignored its master as dogs are given to do when they find something worthy of their interest. Pawing at the heap of leaves and dirt just off the pathway in an idyllic setting, Healy Dell, a beautiful spot of nature on the outskirts of a sprawling greater Manchester town. It was a beautiful, crisp morning and the woman had decided a healthy brisk walk was in order before Bridge club this afternoon. Her cheeks ruddy following a good half mile she was already out of breath. She debated traversing the slippery leaves to retrieve the damn dog and resolved to continue to call her in stern, matronly tones. The woman stood astride the path, hands on hips and for the umpteenth time why this dog was so opposed to obeying her commands. She had taken her to classes, had used the Barbara Woodhouse method of instruction, not particularly favouring the more modern "dog whisperer" type drivel. Yet the dog would not adhere to her rules. A brisk walk in the woods would turn into a battle of wills, the mutt usually coming out top. Terrence, her husband didn't help, he was constantly cooing with the beast, and she knew, although he didn't realise it, that he gave the dogs scraps from the table. She needed to have words with him, more serious words. He was making a rod not for his own but for her back.

Another call, more urgent this time, her ponderings had led her to become a little agitated with the situation, alas "Poppy" was not listening, she was relentless, finding something so enticing that even her master's anger could not distract her from it. Finally the woman gave in, looking around briefly to ensure nobody had seen this flagrant disregard of her authority she caught up with the dog. She was a woman in her fifties, stout and no nonsense, one would expect that her husband, Terrence, would pay her much more attention than the errant Poppy. Despite his furtive attempts to rend the mutt untrainable she was determined that the dog would, eventually be consistently obedient. She wondered why she tolerated the insufferable man at times, times like this, when the simplest of commands became a battle to be fought, and generally lost... She had a distinguished former career in the voluntary sector where her minions did as they were told and God help them if they didn't. A bumbling man and small dog should be the least of her concerns, and yet they were. Anger rising she snapped at the little dog "What have you got there girl?", crouching down to determine what had caught her mutt's attention, she froze for a split second then immediately sprang backwards, arms cart wheeling in a cartoon style flurry, a freakish synchronised swimmer, kicking her heels away from the treasure unearthed by Poppy's excavation. The woman proceeded to hyperventilate, she looked around her, now hoping for a sign of life, of help and support, no one. All thoughts of Terrence's weakness melted from her mind, she needed him here with her. The woods were deserted, no Terrence, no passers-by, no friendly types out for a stroll in the woods. The odd, eerie shriek of a bird and the rustling of leaves on the trees her only company. Not that she would ever admit this at a later date, but she was scared, terrified, the woods took on a terrifying landscape. A dark and anonymous threat lurking behind every tree, every shrub. Fumbling for the mobile phone in her pocket which she would later reveal to friends she had debated taking with her on this fateful walk, she called 999. Poppy, content with her unearthing sat back on her haunches and regarded her mistress, head cocked to one side and appearing to contemplate the seriousness of the situation.

Chapter Nine

The working man's club was a typical 1960's soulless compendium of boxes, seemingly thrown together in a haphazard manner. It had several large square windows that reflected the light in a manner that highlighted the worn, bowed curvature, they threatened to break out at any given moment, adding their shards to those of the broken bottles that were scattered around the perimeter. The building was pebble dashed, most of this had crumbled away, leaving the grey concrete skin exposed. Inside the club it was equally depressing. Paper thin walls covered with nicotine stained paper, there had been no redecoration since the smoking ban in public places had come into force. The club had a large open plan design, typical of most clubs of this type and age. Frayed orange upholstery covered the seating areas which consisted of benches framing the room's outer perimeter and chairs placed opposite, battered Formica tables between them. There was a pool table at the far side of the room, with a ladies and a gents leading off behind, and the bar ran the length of the room to the right of the entrance. A domestic was hoovering the multi coloured "flotex" carpet. When new the carpet would have had vibrant oranges, reds and greens forming an abstract floral design. Years of abuse, however, had rendered the carpet a dull brown with flecks of muted colour and dirt that an industrial cleaner would struggle to remove let alone a hoover. The domestic continued with an industrious air none the less. Making her way around the tables and chairs, appearing to hover over a particularly stubborn piece of dirt every now and then. Despite the ongoing cleaning a few regulars had already made their way into the club, taking up their usual seats, reading the paper, discussing the day's racing form. Pints of warm brown liquid sat on tables in front of them, more a prop or a reason for entry into the club rather than to drink. A radio was playing quietly in the background, relaying information about sporting events, occasionally interspersed with news items. Chink of glass against glass denoted the barman engaged in his work, he halted rubbing the soiled tea towel around a glass that was imparting more dirt than it was extracting and cocked his head when the radio conveyed a useful bit of information and then continued with his work. Despite the decaying nature of the building, it had a certain charm. Perhaps the charm did not lay in the bricks and mortar but rather its inhabitants. The club had an air of community spirit about it, the regulars had a sense of belonging when visiting the place. Arguments would undoubtedly unfold but would equally be resolved, over a warm pint. Dramas, individual and collective would be played out within these walls and this would cement the camaraderie experienced by its members. With the close knit sense of community however, came a deep distrust of strangers. Any new face that dared to enter the club would have to endure a "Slaughtered Lamb" scenario, this would go on for some time. The newbie destined to serve their time and win the trust of the regulars or find somewhere else to drink.

The door opened with a creak and this caused the smattering of men to look towards it. The barman glanced over his shoulder and nonchalantly resumed "cleaning" the glasses. The two small groups of men performed very similar actions, one of them, a man of around fifty with a craggy face that depicted a lifetime of working outdoors, held his glance towards the door for longer than the others. A curious mixture of distaste, wariness and defiance spread across his face, then he too turned to his friend and continued chatting about the latest Leeds United embarrassments.

The focus of this strange lack of attention was a rather large man of around thirty years of age. He strolled up to the bar, seated himself on a stool and leaned forward on both elbows, propping his chin up with fists. He must have been around six foot tall and weighed the best part of eighteen stone. His frame indicated that at one time in his life he would have owned a physique to be proud of. This had given way to a softer exterior with the threat of strength lurking underneath. His movement towards the bar had been slow and deliberate, akin to a Wild West outlaw strutting into a saloon, guns at the ready. He looked up at the barman, neatly trimmed dark hair, a handsome face, ruggedly chiselled features, but the eyes gave away the reception he had received in the club. His eyes were dark, muddy, brown, cold eyes. They conveyed very little other than threat, malice, like the eyes of a snake moving in to strike on a trembling rodent. "A pint of stella when your ready", given his outward appearance, the man had a soft voice, gentle almost. He appeared to have lost most of his Yorkshire accent, it was still there but muted, he may well have travelled. The barman continued to work on his glass for perhaps 30 seconds, he did not turn towards the man while he busied himself with this task. There were furtive glances from the regulars dotted around the club. An air of expectancy seeped through the atmosphere, making it heavy with threat. The barman finally turned towards the hulk of a man sat before him. Without saying a word he pulled a pint of fizzy yellow liquid and thrust it unceremoniously towards him. This caused the liquid to splash over the rim of the glass and onto the bar, narrowly missing the man's elbows. "Sorry about that Dave", the barman stated without an ounce of apology. "That'll be two twenty." with this the barman turned his back and continued to soil clean glasses. Dave slowly raised himself from his seat, rummaged around in his pockets and placed some change quietly onto the counter. He picked up his glass in a bear sized but smooth skinned hand and swaggered over to the furthest corner of the club. There was an audible sigh of relief from one of the regulars. With the threat receding, the soft hum of conversation began to fill the large room

* * *

Dave sat down on a bench, legs splayed in masculine assertiveness. He set down his glass on the chipped Formica table in front of him and then took out a mobile phone from his pocket. Several minutes later he laid his phone down next to his drink and looked out of the window. Watching the steady flow of traffic, eyes flicking to the car park of the club from time to time. He took the occasional sip of his drink, his eyes did not wander around the club and its attendees, they simply looked on at the world outside of the microcosm of the club. Dave's mind began to wander as it often did. He had noticed a woman across the street, she was tall and blond, slim and attractive in a unique sense, eyes slightly too far apart, mouth a little too wide. He thought of Leila, ahh Leila. Dave sighed audibly. Leila had been his angel, his potential salvation. He thought of her not with a fondness but with a growing agitation. He took a long gulp from his beer, checked his phone a couple of times, he did not want to get lost in a reverie, not now. But it was too late. Leila, his love, his sweet, beautiful woman. He believed that she would lift him from the darkness that gnawed away at him... She was kind, she held him close to her as no other female had, she had whispered in his ear and made the demons crawl back into the depths, for a short while at least. They had their ups and downs of course. It took her a while to get used to his tutelage. She had eventually come around to his way of thinking, he had needed her to succumb to him as he was succumbing to her. Or so he had believed. Then the party. Some kind of promotional party for the company she worked for, black tie and the kind of pretentious bullshit that he was neither used to or wanted to be a part of. Leila asked him to "circulate" and she would do likewise. He found himself in front of a fifty something year old woman spouting bollocks about a war he wasn't interested in. Meanwhile, his Leila was "circulating" with a man. Attempting to look interested, holding his glass of bullshit red wine in his hand and focusing with all his might not to crack the elegant wine glass, he nodded, grunted "um" and "ah" in the spaces in between her churning words. He could feel the red mist descending, infusing his brain, making rational thought impossible. The woman's voice seemed to disappear, he was vaguely aware of a mannequin before him, mouth opening and closing, all peripheral sounds and actions disappearing. Just one scene played out in front of him. Leila and the fucking twat of a man she was talking to. His agitation levels were reaching a massive high, he wanted to swipe out every potential distraction to what was going on in front of his very eyes. He analysed the animated exchange, "Really, do you?" "Yes" a slight giggle, biting of the lip, eyes lowered in a coquettish sublimation. Wild gesticulations. She appeared amused, entranced, flirting. Did he see a blush on her cheek? He looked at the mannequin before him, straight through her and walked off in the direction of Leila, managing to knock a few drinks out of the hands of the event goers as he did so. Oblivious to the woman's tuts and exclamations of "How rude", the gasps of those who now wore their drinks he made his way to the back of Leila. He glanced at her, she was wearing a strapless dress, shoulders bare and glinting, a healthy golden tan adorned her soft, velvety skin. Such soft skin, perfect except for a small angry bruise, just beneath her shoulder blade. He was immediately angry. Why was she exhibiting her punishments? The damage to her skin was a symbol of the tuition she was receiving, a private tuition between Leila and himself and for no other to witness.

He had to keep her pure, and she knew this, she understood. He moved in close behind her, stroking her back and at the same time pulling up the dress so that it covered the mark. "Dave, Dave, meet Carl. He works in IT, he's been telling me about all of the mad things you can do on the internet. Carl, this is my partner Dave Cartwright." Leila laughed, was it a nervous laugh, he was guessing yes, it most definitely was. "Time to go Leila" Leila turned around to look at Dave, she looked at him with an expression he hadn't seen before, defiance? "No Dave, it isn't time for me to go." Dave stopped, he was unsure of how to respond, was she actually saying no to him? "OK, Leila, I think you've had enough to drink, we need to go home." He glanced at the poncy Carl and half smiled. Carl looked away from him, non-engaging and clearly not seeing the gravity of the situation. He grabbed Leila by the upper arm "We're leaving" Leila tuned around on him with such force that he was caught off guard, his grip on her loosened. "No Dave, I'm not going anywhere. You go home alone, and I won't be following you. I've had enough of this Dave, I can't take anymore. Don't make a scene, just leave" her voice broke as she uttered the last couple of sentences, but her resolution was clear. She took off through the throng of party goers towards the women's restroom. He was suddenly aware of a quiet bubbling of conversation that was gaining in volume, indication that the room had hushed and witnessed Leila's betrayal. Glancing around Dave realised that he had no option, he had to leave, leave this place and leave Leila with these freaks.. His rage was at boiling point but what could he do? She had floored him. He resolved to make sure she got the punishment she deserved when she came grovelling back home to him. But that didn't happen, he didn't see her again. Unwittingly, Leila had nailed the coffin shut on any humanity Dave had to offer, any potential he may have had for change was lying on the floor, party goers crushing it into the carpet, obliterating it. A fully fledged monster emerged that night, change was now impossible.

* * *

Half an hour past and Dave's demeanour changed, only slightly, he straightened up a little in his seat, brushing an invisible fleck of dust from his jeans. He looked from the car park to the door of the club. A slightly balding middle aged man appeared at the doorway accompanied by the signature creak of the slightly battered door. He glanced around the club, unsure of his surroundings and then he spotted Dave. He bypassed the bar and made directly to where Dave was seated.

His demeanour as he made his way through the club was attempting to be nonchalant, unassuming, but he didn't quite pull it off, he raised a few curious glances from the regulars. He sat down on a worn chair in front of Dave, licking full wet lips nervously, constantly flicking his gaze around him, this man demonstrated the meaning of the word "paranoia", he fidgeted on his seat, eyes darting like a ferret caught in a trap. "Alright Dave" "Alright mate, here you go" Dave leaned forward producing a DVD from his pocket, the

DVD had the words "Candy Man" scrawled across it in black indelible ink. Sliding it across the table and then sweeping back his hand in one movement. In a similar gesture the man retrieved the DVD, secreting it in his own pocket and producing an envelope for Dave. A tainted ritual that any onlooker would have been uncomfortable with, sensing that the exchange contained dark secrets.

Dave checked the contents of the envelope beneath the table, out of view of the other inhabitants of the club. Satisfied he looked up at the man with a smile that exuded darkness, the smile of a hangman that enjoyed his work. "Nice one mate" the soft tone, at odds with the owner of the words. The man did not respond, simply nodded his head as he scrabbled up from his chair and quickly made his way to the exit.

During the course of the next hour more regulars turned up, working men finishing their shifts, an older couple whose ritual involved a pint of bitter and a port and lemon before going home together to prepare the evenings supper. Two more strangers also arrived, singularly, one around fifteen minutes after the other. Both repeated the same transaction as the first only their DVD's bore the scripts "The Terminator" and "Gone with the Wind"

These furtive encounters had not gone unnoticed by the barman. He made his way around the bar clipping the third stranger with his elbow as the man made his way to the door. The barman approached Dave, leaving a slightly nervous stranger to make a quick exit. "What's going on 'ere Dave?" Turning his head slowly from the window to face the barman Dave raised his hands palm up, shrugging his shoulders, a sarcastic, mock hurt expression on his face. "Just selling a few DVD's that I've copied, I've got a pretty decent collection, bit of a film fan to be honest, is there somert you might fancy?" Dave's mouth melted into a sneer. "I don't fancy anything you might be selling, now fuck off before I call the coppers. I don't wanna see you in 'ere again, do we understand each other?" The barman had leaned forward onto the table to impart these words to Dave, tattooed arms were tensed to reveal a formidable muscular form. Dave appeared unperturbed but acquiesced none the less. "Okay, okay" Dave gave a soft laugh as he stood up, the gentle noise escaping his lips juxtaposed to the menacing glare emanating from half closed lids. This combination would cause most to back away, instinctively recognising the threat, but the barman stood his ground, he had dealt with worse situations than this, he wasn't going to let this piece of shit intimidate him. This man gave him the creeps, he'd heard the rumours, not that he believed the half of it, but either way, he wasn't comfortable with this man, he gave off an aura of malice and sickness, and he didn't want him hanging around his club, selling his films, for one second more than he had too.

Dave made his way out of the club in the same manner that he had entered and disappeared from sight, the atmosphere lightened and the close, friendly air returned to settle on the occupants.

Chapter Ten

Anna dropped her office phone onto its cradled. She starred at the phone for several seconds with a solemn expression on her face, the cogs whirring inside her head almost audible. She had taken a call from Gail, the foster carer before getting into work that morning. Gail was concerned, she had noticed bruising around Whitney's thighs. Anna had passed on the time and place of the hospital appointment and Gail agreed to take the little girl. She had sounded upset, she was an experienced foster carer so this had disturbed Anna. Gail had seen lots of children through her doors over the years, they all had their own stories, some more harrowing than others. Gail and her husband Jeff, were able to cope with most situations, it wasn't like her to become emotional. The call Anna had just received explained it all. Looking around the office she located Jean, her hard-nosed manager, Jean might be a real pain in the arse but she was proactive. She made things happen and that was exactly what Anna needed right now. "Have you got a minute?" Jean was in some kind of intense interaction with her PC, tapping away at the keys furiously, nose almost touching the monitor screen, without turning her head she snapped "Does it look like..." "It's important" Sensing the urgency in Anna's voice Jean scooted her wheeled chair away from the PC, short legs struggling to gain a grip on the cheap carpet as she did so. "What's wrong?" Her tone had softened ever so slightly. "The Clayton case, the foster carers escorted the child to an appointment with the paediatrician, it's not good, I think we need to call an urgent meeting" "Who do we need to attend?" Anna was grateful that Jean trusted her judgement enough not have her justify the need for a meeting, Anna needed time to get some information and her head together. "At this point just the police, Charlie might want to attend, he came out with me yesterday." "Right, I'll contact the CPU. I'll let you know what time they can get here. Is it really that bad?" "It is, the paediatrician is faxing over her preliminary report, I'll copy it for you."

For the next hour Anna busied herself printing out reports, assessments and record sheets detailing the link that ran through several cases like a sticky spider's web, Dave Cartwright. She finally collected the fax from the admin desk and then made several copies of all documents, leaving one set on Jean's desk. Back at her desk she scanned the fax. A litany of horrors bestowed on an innocent child. The words on the fax jumped out at her "multiple vaginal lacerations, ruptured cervix, profound haemorrhage, contusion to labia, upper thighs and buttocks, topical infection" on and on went this horrific list, ending simply in the statement "In my opinion these injuries were non accidental in nature." Anna sighed, she leaned forward, elbows on desk and head in her hands. The terrible list, in clinical black and white laid upon the desk equated to the sadistic molestation of an innocent child. Anna was suddenly overwhelmed with sadness, she thought about how this child's life could have been, a sweet and blessed beginning that would create a beautiful, confident and content young woman, equipped to journey into the world with energy and a lust for life. Anna knew all too well that Whitney's future would most likely be filled with post-traumatic stress, self-harm, alcoholism, a string of harmful relationships and years of therapy. If she made it that far. The odds were stacked against her. The sadness was quickly replaced with anger, what gave one individual the right to cause such devastation on the life of another? Anna was convinced that Dave was involved with the other cases. Whitney's wasn't the first life he had destroyed, there must be others. He had to be stopped. Anna's mind conjured up the face of the beautiful, fragile little girl. The look in her eyes constantly on the verge of tears, and yet concealing this horror that she had to live with. How had this child's suffering escaped Anna's notice, there must have been some tell-tale signs? A child could not suffer the injuries she had sustained without any visible indication of her pain. Anna felt nauseous, was it her fault this had occurred, had she missed something, some sign that Whitney had silently attempted to convey? Where was her mother in all of this? What was she doing to protect her "little princess"? Anna could have screamed with the emotions that were boiling inside her, but instead she marched over to Jean's desk, her manager was back in her seat, preoccupied with her computer. "Do we have a time Jean?" Anna asked rather brusquely. True to form, Jean did not look up, "check your emails Anna, two o clock, meeting room three" "Fair enough" Anna replied then turned on her heels to leave the building, she needed some air.

Chapter Eleven

Dave had left the club last night with a pocket full of cash and a smile on his face. He was a little annoyed that he hadn't managed to see all of his customers, but a few text messages later he had managed to reorganise. He had hoped to see a couple of others today, but it could wait. He had plenty of time. He had a busy day ahead of him anyway. The difficulty with his line of work was that for every exquisite high there was an equally unpleasant low. His business today was of the unpleasant kind. Unpleasant business that went by the name of Julie Clayton. He had heard that her beautiful little girl had been taken into care. He needed to make sure that her bitch of a mother didn't talk. He would use his charm, he would convince her that she was as beautiful as her daughter, all the shit that these pathetic women wanted to hear. Then she would be in his pocket, willing to swear black was white for him. This was the unpleasant factor, having to ingratiate himself with ugly, stupid women in order to get to his prize. He did it well though, how many had he duped so far? He couldn't remember, but getting one over on these bitches made him feel like the leader of a cult, the cult of Dave, a smile broke across his face. He called Julie on his mobile and agreed to meet her, engineering the conversation until she believed he was doing her a favour, he was bowing down to her wishes, making her believe that she was the one in control.

The evening was drawing in and he decided to walk the couple of miles to Julie's flat. He knew these streets like the back of his hand, he liked to think of this part of town as his territory. The rows upon rows of stone terraces, long abandoned mills and great stone arched viaducts, all held their secrets. He preferred the darkness, he had no fear walking the streets at night, it was others that needed to fear him. He cut through a narrow winding lane and took a shortcut along the canal, in the diminishing light the water looked like thick, black ink. He passed an abandoned mill, in daylight the mill would bear it's graffitied wounds, scrawls in fluorescent colours of the disaffected youth that congregated at the mill, to drink and use substances. No artwork to adorn the centuries old building, just monikers, dull names that Dave imagined had been sprayed across the walls to alleviate boredom whilst waiting for a dealer to arrive. No Banksys in the making around here. Dave left the anonymity of the canal side to venture onto the road that would lead him to the flats. He passed under a viaduct, the great arch creating a frame around the bustle of shops and a pub ahead of him. He arrived, before ascending the stairs Dave set out a mental list of what he needed to achieve tonight and how to best achieve it. He fixed an almost sheepish smile on his face and then took the stairs two at a time.

* * *

"What 'av you bin doin with that fucking skank!" Dave's greeting was less than salubrious. Dave starred at her for several moments, no expression in his cold eyes, attempting to pin her down, make her still, visual lasso's wrapping their invisible cords around her. "Shall I just leave Julie, I haven't come here for this" Dave responded in a gentle tone, he knew he had her in the palm of his hand. Julie stood back a little from the doorway, hugging herself as she began to cry, snuffles, followed by guttural sobs. Dave stood in the doorway, seemingly oblivious to her emotional crisis, he looked down at his left hand, examined his nails with exaggerated curiosity, then turning away to look at the view from the walkway. Turning back to Julie he asked her "Are you done? You know I don't do all of this Jeremy Kyle shit babe, come on, let's have a chat." Dave stepped through the door way and closed the door behind before Julie had a chance to compose herself. "Why Dave?" The wailing returned. Dave sighed, "OK, c'mon, let's go and sit down, have a chat yeah?" He led Julie into her sparse, dirt ridden living room and sat her down on the sofa, large hands placed around her shoulders. He then took a seat beside her. "What's all this about Julie?" Again, with a soft tone emanating from a form that one would expect expletives and violence from. Julie turned to Dave. "I thought we were ok, I gave you what you wanted" Julie faltered at the last few words, they were coughed out of mouth entwined with breathy sobs. She placed her head in her hands and rocked vaguely back and forth. "They've taken Whitney, my little girl, she's all I have" with this Julie began to wail again, the rocking becoming more pronounced. Dave placed a hand on her knee "Julie, let me tell you what's happened darlin' and then I'll tell you what you're gonna do." Julie responded to these words, hopeful that things were going to be made right, she looked into Dave's eyes imploringly, like a battered dog begging it's owner to hold back a kick.

"Julie, you sold *your little girl* to me for a few quid, you knew what was going to happen, to the law you're as guilty as me for what happened, and you're her mother for fucks sake! What kind of mother would sell their kid like that, you're worse than me. If the law find out about this you'll be the next Myra Hindley. Jesus Julie, what the fuck were you thinking?" Dave paused, allowing his words to sink in. Julie starred ahead, chewing on her bottom lip. "But Dave, I thought we were sound?" "Julie, you're not hearing me, if this gets out we are both in deep shit, but to be honest love, you'll get it worse than me, I've been trying to distance myself from you to keep you safe" Dave regarded Julie and wondered for the first time if he had made a mistake. He prided himself on being able to get these broken, fucked up women to give him what he wanted. He manipulated them into situations they couldn't extract themselves from. By the time they realised what had happened they were in too deep to do anything about it. At this point Julie should be angry, upset with him and desperately to trying to dig herself out of an impossible hole. But not this time, this time this woman was still in love with him, he almost laughed out loud despite himself. What kind of a fucking weirdo was this woman? Not that Dave minded too much, without women like this he wouldn't have such a lucrative business, nor would he be able to satisfy his own needs. He decided that he needed to employ a more harsh method of imposing reality on Julie. "What do you think I paid you for Julie, where has the money been coming from?" Julie shrugged her shoulders, non-committal body language, eyes betraying a sickening guilt. "C'mon Julie, I want to hear you say it, we were in it together babe. What was I paying you for?" Julie whispered something inaudible. "Say it again, I can't hear you." Dave's voice became a little harsher, an air of command seemed to resonate in Julie. "You paid for my Whitney, but I didn't know what yer were doing" the cracked voice again, refusing to say out loud the atrocities she had allowed to happen. "You knew exactly what was happening Julie, you knew I was making videos, not a few cute pictures. What the fuck is wrong with you, you were more than happy to take the cash, you need to take some responsibility for what's happened. I wouldn't have done a thing if you hadn't let me. I fucked your daughter and I filmed it so that we could get some cash together. We could have had a good life together you and me, but you have to fucking spoil everything by going fucking loco on me. Don't you trust me? "Julie looked at him beseechingly, "But you've been fucking around with that other bitch, why?" Dave was caught a little off guard, he had laid down the facts and made it clear what had happened to this woman's daughter. Dave was incredibly confident in his techniques, which he believed he had honed. He fully expected some outrage from Julie, some disgust, hurt, but mainly guilt. This was the emotion that Dave was able to subdue his victims with. But no, Julie was more hurt by his romantic betrayal than by his rape of her six year old daughter. He needed time to think. He didn't know if he was at all associated with Julie by the police. He needed to keep a low profile, the first two had caused him this kind of grief and he had had to deal with it. He felt he had perfected his technique to the point where there was minimal probability that his victims would turn against him. Now he had this problem to deal with. Julie, the woman that had given him his best project yet. "What's going on with the girl then?" Dave asked in a matter of fact manner that resembled him asking about something as banal as the weather. "They've taken her to foster carers, probably the best fucking thing. That bitch of a Social Worker was asking too many questions though. She's a right cow." "Does she know that we are together? What's she called?" "No Dave, no one knows and she's called Anna Black" Julie sighed out the sentence, a realisation that her devastation was going unnoticed. "OK, that's good, is there anyone else you know that might be able to take the blame, if the girl tells anyone what's happened then you might be able to pin the blame on them, what about her dad?" "No Dave, he lives down south, I 'aven't seen 'im for ages, years. I'll think of someone." Julie appeared tired, dejected, finally emotionally battered enough to be able to keep her mouth shut, even though the reasons for her loss of composure were not what he had planned. Dave grew in confidence at the rate that Julie's disintegrated. Dave finally felt able to leave the situation in control. She wasn't going to say anything, she needed a bit of time to stew, let his harsh words sink in, fully appreciate just how deep she was implicated in this. He would offer her some succour and then disappear, abandon her, crank up her anxieties. "What about a couple of beers, eh? I'll nip down to the offy and get a few. We'll have a quiet night in?" "I don't know Dave, I'm tired. Why don't yer come back tomorrow? I need to think." Dave felt an unease surging through him for the second time, what was going on here? Why didn't he know exactly what was going through this woman's head? He forced his anxieties to the back of his mind, this woman was an oaf, an almost illiterate idiot that was not averse to selling her own child into pornography. He was a million light years beyond her, in intellect, cunning and intuition. He could leave her to stew in her own juice for a couple of days, he decided that no woman, of inferior intellect or otherwise would go to the authorities to implicate themselves in the sexual molestation of their own flesh and blood. With that he made a hasty retreat, with promises to call around to the house for a chat in a couple of days. As soon as Dave was out of the front door he drew out his mobile phone, setting up a rendezvous for the sale of his remaining DVD's.

* * *

Internet on, he looked up Kirklees Social Services, obviously he wouldn't be able to find out exactly which office Anna Black worked at but he should be able to find the building. And there it was, Children and Family Services, the offices were based on a leafy street on the outskirts of Huddersfield. There was a telephone number listed, could it be this simple. Punching the number in he listened to the recorded message. No, he didn't have Anna Black' extension number, yes he would wait for the operator. An extremely curt voice "Children and Family Services, can I help you?" the voice did not project the motivation to help anyone, he smiled. "Could I speak with Anna Black please?" "Who's calling?" That was all he needed, she obviously worked in that building, he hung up. Julie had given him a pretty good description, although there were likely to be several dark haired thirty odd year olds working at that office. Julie hadn't been too sure of the car, she knew it was small and silver.

Dave boarded a 316 bus, he paid his fair and chose a seat by the window. He preferred to travel by bus, he could drive and could afford a car, but he enjoyed the experience, he liked to immerse himself in the human detritus that could be found in plentiful amounts using this mode of transport. He was always on the lookout for a new project and who knew what he would chance upon on a bus. Eventually disembarking at a stop closest to the Social services building, he strolled along the road. From this vantage point he could see the car park, now it was a case of finding somewhere to wait. He lit a cigarette and scanned the street. A taxi rank, several fast food restaurants that were closed due to the time of day, a florist, a corner shop and an avant garde cafe. He wandered across the road and made as if to look at the menu, a few stainless steel tables and chairs were placed in front of the cafe, he glanced over his shoulder and noted that he could see the car park of the Social Services building from this vantage point.

"A coffee please darlin'", "What kind of coffee would you like sir?" The girl, probably no older than eighteen, not the most confident ambassador of the service industry, she struggled to make eye contact with the large man before her. Dave exhaled and leaned forward on the counter top, the cafe was deserted, he, the only patron and it would seem she the only staff. "A coffee kind of coffee love." His face was opposite hers, an unblinking stare and a fixed, unnerving smile on his face. The girl turned away and busied herself making an Americano it would seem. He could have fun here but decided against, the last thing he wanted was to draw attention to himself. He paid for his coffee with a wink and a thank you, the girl forced a smile and found something extremely important to do at the back of the counter.

He took a seat outside of the cafe offering him the best vantage point of the car park. He whiled away the time smoking, sipping on his coffee, amusing himself with daydreams. Several people entered and existed the building he was surveying, and finally his patience paid off. It was now late in the afternoon, probably knocking off time. A dark haired woman came out of the building. She was with a male, a colleague? They stood at the front of the building for a while, chatting. She then moved off into the car park and hallelujah! Opened a small silver Peugeot 107. Dave stood abruptly, deciding to seize the moment. He made his way a couple of doors down to the Taxi Rank. He had commandeered a taxi within a minute, business was clearly slow at this time of day. Once in the cab, he claimed that he didn't know the address of his destination but knew how to direct that cabbie. This was alarmingly accepted with a nod of the head "Go for it pals." Dave muttered for a while until the Peugeot pulled out of the car park. He then set about the task of following Anna Black to her home, her place of refuge, or so she thought.

Chapter Twelve

The "SOCO'S" had taken some time to excavate the remains, thirty six hours in all, working day and night. The setting of the final resting place was an attraction to hoards of members of the public, out to walk their dogs, jog, and a stroll on a particularly clement afternoon. The police tape and stark white tent surrounding the scene was enough to disturb a good portion of these civilians, creating an association with the unsafe, it would be months, years in some cases before they would return here, and even then with caution, not alone. The fruits of the Scene of Crime officers labour were two skeletons, one an adult, one a child of around six, both female, both lives extinguished at the hands of another. Remnants of clothing remained intact, difficult to determine due to the build-up of grime from time spent under the earth. The smaller skeleton was lying face down on top of the larger, in what appeared to be an embrace. A child clinging onto her mother for all eternity. Head buried into what would have once been a breast. The scene was difficult for some of the officers to process and a heavy quiet soaked with sadness surrounded the scene of crime. Officers performed their task meticulously, all wanting to ensure that any evidence of who had perpetrated this crime would be carefully tagged, bagged and preserved. The Greater Manchester area had it's fair share of serious crimes, including murder, some of the most infamous crimes in Britain had been committed within the district. This did not detract from the sheer tragedy of what lay before them, in a cold, shallow grave. The terrible history of the place did not harden these officers to the inhumanity of the crime that had been committed, rather each that had a sister, a mother, a child considered their own security and that of their loved ones. None the less, they carried out their respective roles with diligence and professionalism.

The DI leading the case looked at the evidence before him. The perpetrator did not appear to be particularly "forensically aware". A hammer appeared to be the weapon that had caused the deaths of the two victims, this had been casually thrown into the makeshift grave, in addition to a rotted yet salvageable shred of fabric that the larger of the two skeletal remains still grasped within bony fingers. The fabric did not match any of the remnants of clothing belonging to the deceased. Another significant find was a plastic carrier bag containing a number of DVDs, with any luck the IT geeks would be able to pull something from them which would give them a lead. The DI believed that despite the degraded state of the remains, there would be enough clues to determine how these two unfortunate lives had been cut short, and by whom. Why this had happened, in his experience, would be a much more difficult concept to grasp. Despite the reasoning behind the many murder cases he had been involved in he had never been able to reconcile the sheer pointlessness of inflicting death on another. Senseless acts of predation belonged in the animal kingdom, some would argue that at their base level all humans are merely animals, but he disagreed, how could a species capable of so much beauty, creativity, compassion and empathy have any reason to commit such atrocious acts? A hobby that doubled as a therapeutic outlet for his day job was classical music. He enjoyed nothing more than to listen to the heart rending Vitali Chaconne or an earth moving Wagner. These composers were human, made of the same kind of DNA, same molecular and biological structure as the sadistic offenders he had to deal with. On late nights, with a glass of good malt in hand he would sit in his conservatory, gaze at the stars and contemplate the meaning of things, his life, his sordid world. He had no answers of course, for there were none. His conclusion had simply been, for whatever reason this planet had dictated, some individuals were simply bad. He wasn't a religious man but he firmly believed in evil, bad not mad was the main conclusion of his 26 years in the force. He had come across victims of crime who had been subject to the same forces that created their perpetrators; there was no rhyme or reason. Why one and not the other? There were of course the academic theories. A sequence of bad parenting, knock on the head, etc etc, being refused a second ice cream whilst on holiday to the Caribbean for all he knew. The simple truth was there was no truth. It was unpredictable. As much as the academics would like to tag, label and pigeon-hole each violent offender, he, and his colleagues knew, it was so much bullshit.

On this night his contemplations were a little more upbeat. For good or bad this was the career he had chosen and he would methodically lead his team to painstakingly sift through the evidence, leads, interviews, hours in front of computer screen to bring some justice to this case. He was as stoic as he was perplexed by human nature. He had returned home tonight, chatted with his wife, recalled some mundane anecdote from his day, asked the children how their schoolwork was coming along. The small things mattered, kept him grounded, his wife would never know how much her chattering about the small "p" politics of working in a florist contributed to his sanity, and he loved her for it. He glanced at his watch, ten thirty, time to retreat into a restless sleep.

* * *

A pink plastic mac with tiny black elephants printed in a random pattern across sleeves and collar had faired well despite years of burial. It was the mac, along with various other pieces of clothing, the tatters of a checked Marks and Spencer's shirt, Nike trainers, tiny pink sparkly wellington boots and an unusual piece of jewellery that had possibly identified the forlorn souls in the makeshift grave as Karen and Emily Osborne. As expected, painstaking research, trawling though databases, hundreds of phone calls had located the evidence that led to a couple of missing person's reports six years ago. As luck would have it the filer of one of the reports, sister and aunt of the deceased had been able to provide descriptions of clothing worn when her loved ones had last been seen, and they were identical to the remnants of clothing worn by the victims.
Now the hard part. Contacting the family, having them view the last remaining items associated with their slaughtered loved ones and making a positive ID. It was the worst part of the job, but part of the job that needed to be done. The DI decided he would tag along on this particular task himself, ideally he would delegate, but for some reason he felt the need to remain in contact with the front line. To experience the difficulties that his

officers had to face, and more importantly to identify with the victim. He was well aware that some of his younger officers felt that he was keeping tabs, not allowing them to develop both their responsibilities and careers. But he felt differently, he would soon be retired and a replacement who was more in tune with the needs of these young officers would take the helm, where to he didn't like to speculate on. In the meantime he felt that he needed to show his officers what he believed to be the right manner to conduct investigations. He hoped he imparted on the emerging investigators how to add some humanity to the end product of a vicious and cruel end, to know what the victims were like as human beings, listen to anecdotes, see the tears of those who had loved them, who would continue to mourn their loss. The younger officers preferred a method of detachment, compartmentalising, they had not lived life enough or travelled closer towards an understanding of their own mortality to appreciate the need to value each and every life that they had encountered the demise of. This did not concern him. Even though he knew intrinsically that each case he worked on took away a little of himself he was sure that his methods contributed to his success rate. Ultimately that was his goal, to solve crimes and provide some peace to the remaining, living victims. This was something he did well and hoped that his progeny would take at least a little of this with them into their own careers.

Chapter Thirteen

Anna sat back on her coach, sinking in to the chenille softness of the furniture, an upholstery hug. Her thoughts sifting through the events of the day. The meeting had gone well, the police appreciating the evidence she had laid before them. Dave Cartwright, seducer of women and molester of children was now on the radar, Anna felt little comfort in this. She had returned from work, called an old friend for a catch up, watched a particularly well made film, eaten her favourite snacks, but nothing could detract her from the ill feelings she had around this case. It wasn't just about the horrors the child had endured. There was more to it. Anna felt that this was just the tip of the iceberg. What had happened to the other families Dave had been associated with? Two of the women had dropped completely off the radar. Anna needed to find out more. She would start tomorrow by contacting the women that were still around. The police had promised to interview Julie Clayton about her daughter's injuries and would gather some information regarding David Cartwright. As he was a schedule one offender the police database would have information regarding his registered address and various other details. They had decided to speak with Julie in the first instance, to determine if there were any other men that had access to Whitney. The paediatrician had stated that the injuries were fairly recent, although some of the internal wounds were beginning to heal they had all occurred within the previous month. The video interview would be booked in order to capture Whitney' statement, such as it would be, as the corporate parent, the social services department did not need to obtain Julie Clayton's consent for an interview to take place. The evidence obtained from Whitney was crucial, but more importantly the interviews needed to take place quickly so that the girl could then access some kind of therapy and try to move on. With any luck adoptive parents would be found for her and some semblance of normality could be injected into her life. Anna desperately hoped that this would be the case, but she doubted it.

Anna packed away her laptop and considered calling Charlie to bounce ideas. It was late and he was likely to be in bed. She could perhaps text him. If he was awake that would be ok, he could always choose to ignore her. If asleep he wouldn't even know. Picking up her phone, she pulled up his details, "I have some thoughts on the Whitney case, are you awake?" The text message simple, to the point. She was about to lay the phone down on the coffee table, it beeped. Good old Charlie.

Half an hour later he turned up to her house, the pretext was the case, the undertones carried a note of embarrassment but hope of a reconciliation in Anna's case, a chance to get their friendship back on track. Charlie fostered a similar sense of embarrassment but also the hope that she may have changed her mind. They discussed the case for a while, Anna went over the plan, asked how he had got on with Julie. Conversation turned to a more casual note, then she blurted it out, it was there, in the ether, hanging like a heavy swinging pendulum in the space between them. "The other day

Charlie..." He looked away from her, clearly embarrassed. "Charlie, look at me, it's not that I don't like you, quite the opposite, it's just we work together, you know?" After a long silence Charlie leaned over to Anna and kissed her, she didn't resist.

* * *

Dave calmed himself, he was crouched in Ann's front garden, had been watching her work on her computer for some time. He was particularly enchanted by the serious way in which she was viewing whatever she was viewing on the screen. It amused him, a busy little bee, she seemed strong, the expressions on her face, the leaning in, the frantic note taking. A focused woman, he liked it. What he liked even more was that she appeared to be on her own. Until some guy showed up. It was late, too late for visitors, perhaps he lived with her husband, boyfriend, but no, he actually rang the doorbell. If he lived there he would have a key, surely. Dave had heard his car pull up and had settled himself into a hedge of shrubs, facing away from the house, hoping that his dark clothing and hair would blend into the night. It appeared to work, Anna Black opened the door and the guy went inside. He maintained his position for some time and when finally convinced that he not been seen he walked slowly over to the window.

He watched them, the normality of the scene was almost sickening to him. They chatted away, oblivious of the alternate reality that played out around them. The pain and suffering that others endure, have to endure to maintain the balance of things. Then things started to get interesting, Dave admonished himself for not having the foresight to bring a camera with him, it had been spur of the moment, he wasn't expecting a show. He quickly took out his mobile and set the camera to video. Anna and Charlie made decent models, he captured their eager, passionate lovemaking, to his surprise it was more exploratory than he would have imagined. Well done Anna, Dave felt he had made a connection with her. She needed to star in one of his films, he could really explore what she was capable of, unlike this goon, Anna was taking the lead, she knew how to excite an audience, unwittingly of course.

Pleased with the fruits of his labour he made his way home. Anna had started out as an annoying, meddling bit player, his original plan had been to intimidate, to frighten off, but things had taken a sudden turn... He was flexible, adaptable, and judging by the performance he had witnessed tonight it would seem that she was following in his footsteps. He just needed to get the timing right, if she were to do anymore digging around then she might make a connection to other women, he couldn't allow that to happen. She would be providing the coppers with info before he could execute an exit plan. Now Dave had a very different role for Anna, he wanted her in one of his films. She would be a difficult one to lure but he was confident that he'd be able to come up with something. What a night, fortune smiles on the brave, Dave knew this to be true. The lovely Anna, she was in for a real treat, she was about to discover a new religion, very soon she would be worshipping at his alter.

Chapter Fourteen

He had managed to sell another three DVD's, changing the location of his office from the working men's club to the bus station. He wasn't particularly happy with the exposed location but business was business. At two hundred quid a pop he had notched up twelve hundred today, not a bad days work, and there were plenty more customers in need of a hard-core specialist viewing such as the ones he provided. He had customers who were prepared to pay a bit extra for a tailored DVD. Blue eyed and blond haired, Chinese, chubby, sky blue pink, there was no accounting for taste. Dave did what he could to satisfy consumer demand. His latest project was mixed race, mother white and father Jamaican. A mocha skinned, green eyed beauty he had come across outside the Salvation Army. Her mother, who had clearly been strung out on some upper or another had been arguing with a worker at the army, attempting to acquire a food parcel, the third that month and definitely not allowed according to the bible bashing middle aged woman that had seen it all before. The argument ended with the Salvation Army worker crisply turning on her heels with a final "No!" and allowing the self-locking door to slam in the mothers face. "So much for charity eh love?" Dave had approached the woman and her daughter. "Too fucking right man!" Exclaimed mum, marching up and down in front of the army doors as if to burrow a tunnel into the building. "Look, I'm not being funny, but I've been there, where you are now, why don't I take you and your lovely daughter for some food?" Dave had stepped away, holding up his hands, palms up "I don't want anything, but you and the kid need a meal, it's on me, what do you think?" The woman had looked momentarily suspicious, had glanced down at her daughter then smiled a glorious, substance enhanced smile exposing slightly yellow teeth. "Yeah, why not?"

That was how it started, a random act of kindness. The woman, as they all were in some way or another, was oblivious to the fact that Dave had one eye on their offspring, appraising, placing a value on them as if they were fattened calves ready to be sold to the slaughter house. Dave would never be able to understand these women, their stupidity, selfishness, greed. He believed that they deserved the pain and guilt that they endured after he had got what he wanted from them, if they endured it at all. And those that attempted to protest, well they also got what they deserved. They were victims of their own gullibility. He was just a conduit, providing a service to those who were willing to pay, if he enjoyed the process then so what, these little bitches would turn into whores just like their mothers anyway, he was helping them along, bringing a little reality into their lives, giving them a head start. Dave had arranged to see the woman, Sharon, this evening, she had been texting him all day, texts full of innuendo, laden with x's, like a teenage girl high on her first brush with romance. She was typical of the woman he befriended, attention seeking and compliment starved, not particularly attractive, broken. The kind that was easy to manipulate and even easier on which to lay the guilt, blame even. The kind that would keep their mouth shut after the deed was done.

And of course she had a photogenic daughter. Dave had been seeing her for a couple of months, making sure he had a new business venture before tidying up the old one. She was hooked, he was almost ready to make his move, tonight would be the night he planted the seed. The narcotics that Sharon craved wouldn't be as forthcoming as on previous liaisons, he would feign a deal gone bad, lack of funds but a sure fire way of getting the cash rolling in again. He didn't think that she would take much persuading, it was as if the girl didn't even exist when he was around, she was a minor annoyance to her mother at best. Sharon had one friend in life, drugs, Dave came a close second as a supplier of the means to get hold of the said drugs. All else was irrelevant to Sharon, her dignity, her past, her future, her child.

Sharon opened the door to her grubby, claustrophobia inducing house as if she were welcoming her teen idol. "Hiya!" the excitement in her voice made Dave internally recoil. Outwardly he beamed at Sharon, taking in her form, she was thin to the point of anorexia, sharp collar bones jutting out and forming a "v" above the tight tee shirt she was wearing, arms poking through the sleeves appeared to belong to a malnourished child. Her tee shirt reminded him of some long forgotten memory, a caricatured cow was emblazoned across the front of the washed out, grey shirt, he wasn't sure why but his mood shifted slightly. He had been upbeat on his way over here, plenty of money in his pocket and anxious to start his new venture. For some reason the image of Sharon stood before him had thrown him a little off kilter, a little less able to focus on the task at hand. He attempted to shrug off the feeling, "Hiya darlin', good to see yer". He draped a large arm around her shoulders and pulled her towards him, almost suffocating her, Sharon reciprocated, throwing her arms around his formidable girth, unable to make her hands meet around his frame. Sharon was skittish in his embrace, like a tiny bird making a feeble attempt to dislodge itself from a net. Dave knew she was craving the hard stuff. The disconcerting thoughts that had crept into his head dissipated as quickly as they had arrived and he set his mind to the task in hand.

* * *

They settled down onto the sofa, Sharon had made a pathetic attempt at laying out some food, a grotesque cocktail party, she had placed crisps and diced cheese into chipped dishes on a small table in front of the sofa. Alongside the bowls were bottles of cheap beer no doubt purchased from a European supermarket. A small lamp threw off a weak orange glow in the corner of the room, casting elongated shadows in it's wake. A CD was playing, some dated "madchester" band, drawling words to a simple yet effective guitar riff. Dave leaned over and picked up a crisp from the dish, he held it in front of his face, eyes poring over the snack as though it were a rare and seldom seen delicacy, he smiled at Sharon, offering his approval. Taking a bite he then offered the remainder to her, she opened her mouth to take the nibble, giggling and shuffling in her seat as she did so. "Have you got anything else for me Davey?" she asked with mock coyness, chewing on the crisp whilst she spoke. Dave felt revulsion at her eagerness, but he remained smiling, "I have babe, but not much. I told you about a guy I was doing business with yeah? Felix? Well the fucker has let me down big time. I swear, if it didn't mean that I'd get sent down I'd have slit his fucking throat. But that 'd mean I wouldn't get to see you babe." Dave paused for effect. His appraisal of Sharon noted slight panic fading to relief and ending with, what? Pride? He wasn't entirely sure but it was a positive response. One that he was hoping for. "It's really fucked me over Shaz. I'm not sure what I'm gonna do about it. I've got people that need supplying, do yer know what I mean? They are not gonna be happy with me." Sharon shuffled around on the sofa a little and reached out to hold Dave's face in her hands, she pulled his it towards hers, her eyes flickering over her face that had he held her gaze for too long it would have made him giddy. "Don't worry babe, we'll think of something" Despite her words being aimed at consoling Dave Sharon's body dictated her own need, she was beginning to fidget in the chair, constantly chewing her bottom lip, eyes darting towards his pockets each time she thought he was looking in a different direction. Dave saw his cue, he slowly pulled himself forward and simultaneously dipped into his pocket to retrieve a packet. Setting the packet down on the table he proceeded to lay out the paraphernalia that would ensure Sharon's happiness, at least for the next few hours. Dave, however wasn't interested in her happiness, he was interested in her state of mind now, he knew that she had a craving gnawing it's way right through her belly, making her nerve endings react to the slightest stimulus, making it hard for her to focus on anything other than the all-consuming hunger she was feeling at this precise moment. It was at this moment that he could get her to do anything he wanted her to do.

But these women were unpredictable, he had learned that it didn't always go as planned, he had found himself surprised at the strength of the maternal protection of offspring at times. So he had devised a new MO. He liked to test the waters first, just an idea, plant the seed so to speak and see what the reaction was likely to be before the real fun began. He had high hopes for Sharon but tonight would be the acid test. As Dave leisurely toyed with the crack on the table Sharon was on the edge of her seat, she slid off the sofa and kneeled in front of the table, watching Dave's hands work his magic. "I know this guy, he's a bit of a weirdo, into homemade porn films, that kind of stuff" Sharon nodded attentively, eyes never leaving the powdered paradise on the table. "If I were to make something he goes for then we could make a killing there. It'd get me out of the shit I'm in and would keep you in this stuff for as long as you wanted". Another nod from Sharon and Dave wondered if she was literally salivating. "Do you think you could be up for somert like that Shaz?" Back to reality, this last sentence required an answer "Erm, yeah why not, what would I have to do?" "I don't think you'd have to do very much at all Shaz, he's into kids, probably a few photos, nothing serious, I wouldn't want any harm coming to your little Kelly" Shaz shifted uncomfortably on her knees, if she was feeling any revulsion or horror at what had just been suggested it didn't register on her face. Dave held the pipe to his mouth and lit it, taking in a long, slow drag, holding in the smoke before exhaling in Sharon's direction, he slumped back into the sofa, holding onto the pipe. Sharon was clearly struggling to contain herself "Yeah, yeah, a few photos eh, what's the harm in that, no probs" Dave rewarded Sharon with the pipe, she quickly and expertly lit it from beneath drawing on the substance that would transform her world into something bearable. A satiated smile spread across her face and she crawled onto the sofa with Dave curling herself into his frame like a cat in front of a warm, open fire. Dave realised that this was phase one, if, when Sharon emerged from her stupor she was still on board with his suggestion he knew he had her in the palm of his hand. If not he would move on, there seemed to be an abundance of rejects that could fill his orders.

Chapter Fifteen

Anna steeled herself for the day ahead with a mug of strong, black coffee. It was early, she had had a fitful night's sleep and woke just a little less tired than she had felt before getting into bed. Anna decided to work from home, she had emailed the admin and her manager to advise them that she was going to catch up on paperwork. She didn't want Jean's watchful eye catching her looking up old files that related to Dave Cartwright. Jean would point out, and rightly so, that investigating all angles was now the remit of the police. Anna didn't feel she could trust the police to investigate as fully as they should, budget cuts, paperwork that equalled her own and diminishing staffing often led to cases such as this not getting the input they deserved. The Child Protection Unit of the police department consisted of a whopping three and a half full time staff, apparently speed camera vans and staking out shopping centres was a more worthy police pursuit than investigating horrific crimes such as this. So, she would do it herself. The police were focussing on speaking with Julie, and then hopefully with Dave Cartwright, if she were to present additional information to them then it would hopefully increase the scale of the investigation and transfer to CID. Anna knew that there was more to this case and public spending dictated that she had to provide the evidence.

* * *

She opened her laptop in order to access the social services database, deciding that the best place to start would be the historical records. The two women who had left the area were the logical starters. If the police were to progress their next step, it would be to contact the women who had been known to Dave and who remained up to date on the social services records. Anna pulled up the most recent of the women who had fled. Karen Osborne, date of birth 1976, one daughter Emily Osborne, known to social services due to Karen's penchant for alcohol, drugs and leaving her child unattended. There were no care orders but the social worker on the case was recommending that the child be removed from the mother's care. The last record entry before the case was put on hold was matter of fact, emotionless, an example of a worker with too much to do and little time to do it: "Visit to Karen at agreed time of 3:30 pm, Karen DNA'd, call to parents, they stated Karen had decided to move out and live with current boyfriend, Dave. They said she would be in touch when settled, Parents could not give any more info although it is unlikely from what I know of Karen that she would have told her parents where she was going. Grandparents have good attachment with Emily. Further t/c to grandparents, Karen has not been in touch, discussion in supervision with manager, case to be stacked until further notice." And that was it, a worker too busy to hear the clanging of alarm bells. "Stacking" the case is a phrase used to describe those cases that won't get any attention unless a call comes in, an emergency needs to be dealt with. In other words, abandoned.

Still, the worker had scrupulously recorded the names, addresses and telephone numbers of all concerned in the case. Anna had three to concentrate on, mum and dad and a sister that had been Karen's staunchest advocate. Providing her with the support and encouragement that Karen and her daughter desperately needed. Records detailed the sister, Laura, attending meetings, taking care of Emily, ensuring that Karen attended her therapy sessions, fighting for the doomed relationship between mother and daughter. She was a key figure in Karen's life and Anna felt that she may know something about Karen's disappearance.

There was a landline recorded in the records, Anna hesitated for a split second before she punched the number into her cheap work's mobile. The line rang a few times and Anna was surprised when a woman answered "hello" The word was pronounced as two "Hell O" in the manner that a secretary or receptionist would utter the word. The voice was clipped and bereft of the Yorkshire twang, Anna was briefly confused and assumed she had dialled the wrong number "Er, hello, I'm sorry I was trying to get hold of a Laura Cassidy" "Yes, Laura speaking?" Anna attempted to keep the surprise from her voice "Hello Laura, my name is Anna Black, I'm calling from Social Services. I wonder if you have a few minutes to talk?" "What's this about?" Laura's tone was clipped and unfriendly, Anna knew that this was going to be a tough call. "This is about your sister, Karen. I'm trying to find out where she is, I need to speak with her regarding another matter and hoped you might be able to tell me where she is. Would it be OK for me to visit for a chat?" Anna always felt better with face to face contact, there were more opportunities to build up a relationship, as brief as the relationship was. "I don't know where she is so I'm not sure I'll be able to tell you anything." Again, the clipped tone, a distrust of social services that Anna had heard in so many voices. "Laura, I would really appreciate it if you would see me, any information would be important, I won't take up too much of your time," Perhaps Laura heard the earnestness in Anna's voice, she relented "Well, I'm free later on this morning, around 11 o'clock, but I need to leave the house by twelve," "That's great, thank you." Anna relayed this with a sincerity and relief that was audible through the telephone network. Laura's tone softened slightly as she provided Anna with her details. Anna jotted down Laura's address and ended the phone call. She assumed that as Laura didn't know where her sister and niece were she was happy to receive a visit from anyone that may be able to help, even if it did involve dancing with the devil that was social services.

* * *

Eleven o'clock, which gave a couple of hours to trawl through the extensive records that were in some way related to Dave Cartwright. It would be like looking for a needle in the proverbial haystack. Social services databases are not the easiest to negotiate. Each case had it's own set of files and documents were frequently filed under the wrong headings, so "Correspondence" may well turn up under the header "Referral." To be sure she didn't miss anything

Anna would have to trawl through each header, of which there were around thirty, and under each header there could be hundreds of documents. Two hours wasn't enough when she had in total six cases to go through. Another coffee on the go Anna sighed, deciding to stick with Emily's case. She had a meeting with the mother's sister but this may prove fruitless. She needed to dig further. She eventually came across an Emergency Duty Team report. The document related an incident between Emily's mother and her partner, name unknown. A neighbour had called to state there was a disturbance at the Osborne residence. The neighbour was concerned that the child, who was known to Social Services, was in danger. The police as well as EDT had attended. The upshot being that Karen, appearing to be a little under the influence had stated she and her partner had a barney over his infidelity. She had asked him to leave, he had, she refused to give his name, but revealed that he lived on Kennel Bank Road, exactly which number she did not know. The house and child were checked out, all was OK and that was the end of the incident. The date on the record indicated that this occurrence had taken place around six months before Karen left the area, and 4 months before Dave's name showed up as her partner. Could this be the same man? Kennel Bank Road was not the most salubrious area of town. It was one of those strange streets that was at once leafy and green, with wild woods to the backs of the long row of stone built Victorian villas, but just a little too close to town for comfort, most of the houses had long ago been turned into bedsits, a sanctuary for those down on their luck, or wanting to drop out. It would be easy to find a bedsit that didn't require references and rent was by the week, cash in hand. The area was at once idyllic and unsettling. The kind of place a sleaze like Dave Cartwright would hole up.

Anna made a quick phone call to the police officer assigned to the case. On the pretext of updating her records she obtained a description of Dave, dropping the tiniest of hints that she may have more information available from a relative, from one of the historical cases he was associated with, nothing major, and then quickly asking what progress our fine members of the constabulary had made on the case. The answer was, in short very little. Julie wasn't saying anything, she was acting the tight lipped, anti-authority hard case one minute, and the hysterical, bereft mother the next. Demanding that the police "do their fucking job and find out who did this to my baby!" Anna and the officer she was conversing with exchanged sighs, both conveying the weariness they found in dealing with the detritus of society. Anna thanked the officer for his time and requested that she be updated with any developments. A MAPPA meeting had been set for next week. This was to look at the risk that Dave Cartwright, manipulator of women and molester of children, may impose on a vulnerable and unsuspecting public. She said she would be there and hoped they had more to go on this time next week.

So, she had a description, a possible location. Anna wasn't adverse to a little homework. Perhaps she needed to find out a little more about Mr Cartwright and what he was up to now he had moved on from Julie. Julie..., Julie, why hadn't she given the police more to go on? Did she not feel any guilt for allowing a monster into her life, allowing access to her most precious of possessions? What kind of a hold did this monster manage to wrap around this woman and others like her. Was he that terrifying or so much of a prize that they were willing to offer innocent sacrifices to his alter? If only Julie would admit to what she knew, the police would have enough evidence to bring him in and it could prevent another horror. There was DNA evidence found on the poor child, but this would take time to analyse, it would also mean matching up the DNA with the perpetrator. Real life in a northern British town was not like CSI, it took weeks to get back the results, not an hour. Anna suddenly remembered the way that Charlie had built up an easy and forthcoming rapport with her. She decided to give Charlie a call and pass on details of the PO that was dealing with the case. Perhaps they could utilise him in an interview with Julie. It was worth a try.

Chapter Sixteen

Charlie clicked the red phone icon on his mobile. He contemplated the conversation that had just taken place. Anna had yet again enticed him into taking on more work than he had the time, or the motivation to do. How did she manage to manipulate him, again? The question left him with a faint smile on his face. He could imagine being manipulated by others far less beguiling than Anna. He liked her, in addition to having a professional admiration for her, but at the same time, he had his own work and pressures that he needed to attend to. As a fledgling social worker he was acutely aware of the reputation he needed to build for himself. This wasn't just an office politics situation, it was with the other professionals he came into contact with, including the police. He supposed a difficult case like this wouldn't do any harm to his credibility with the CPU. He was also horrified by the facts that had emerged during the course of Anna's investigations into the case. He had Julie down as a stray sheep that needed returning to the flock, it had turned out that she was potentially a herd leader. It would seem he had a lot to learn. He would, of course, do what he could to help the investigation move forward but couldn't help feeling a little annoyed, a little proud perhaps. That Anna had drawn him into a case that was probably way above his level of experience.

Picking up the phone he contacted the DC that was leading the investigation, he arranged a visit to Julie's home address, the police had nothing to hold her on and she had been returned to her sad flat with minimal furniture in a depressing and dark world he had fortunately never had to experience first-hand. Good, the values were returning. Rather than feeling like a pawn in a game of social services versus reckless parent chess he felt that he may be able to assist the situation. Bring it to some conclusion. He knew that he had a good rapport with people, perhaps Julie would shed some light on what she felt may have happened to her daughter.

Chapter Seventeen

Glancing at the digital grey display in her car Anna noted that she had ten minutes to get to Laura's house, she should make it, the traffic was pretty quiet at this time of day. She took a left off the main road and made her way along a wide, leafy street, a golf course hidden behind oak and maple on one side and some very pleasant abodes with long driveways, manicured lawns and polished door furniture. Fixby was one of the nicest areas of the town in which Anna lived and worked. It was aspirational living for the few that arrived here. A few miles out of the town centre and enough greenery to give the impression of semi-rural living. Anna was impressed. A couple of minutes later she took another left onto a small side street. There was a row of immaculately kept stone cottages, originally she guessed there may have been ten, possibly twelve. Now, however, she only counted three front doors.

As she got out of the car a woman appeared at the door of the end cottage, the suspicious, affronted look in her eye, crossed arms, head thrown back a little forcing her to look down on Anna, indicated this must be Laura,

Anna locked the car and made her way down the shingle pathway leading to the cottage. Anna held out her hand to Laura and began "Hiya, I'm Anna, we spoke..." Laura glanced down at the proffered hand as if it were covered in dog faeces, ignoring it she interrupted "Yes, yes, come in, I don't have long".

Anna followed her into the house, it was homage to Laura Ashley, an abode that would have been at home in a glossy magazine, and an estate agent would have described it as "deceptively spacious". From outside the cottage was not particularly tall, just about squeezing two floors in the squat structure, however what the home lacked in height it gained in width. "Sit down please" Laura motioned to an overstuffed, floral sofa and Ana complied. She needed to get this woman on board. Laura's tones were clipped and typical of an acquired middle class Yorkshire accent. All vowels and consonants sounded but with the twang still embarrassingly present. Anna quickly surveyed her surroundings, taking in the details that would allow her to communicate more effectively with Laura. The back wall of the room had a delicately carved sideboard that appeared almost Moroccan in style, it covered a large portion on the wall and was flanked by an elegant brass floor lamp topped with a tasselled, powder blue shade and an ornately engraved hall chair. Above the sideboard were various black and white photos, in frames of different shapes and sizes but with a uniform dark wood, this gave a sense of design rather than randomness. The photos were of family scenes, some could have come with the original packaging with the frame and be of no relation to the woman in the room at all. A little girl in a pretty white summer dress, obviously squealing with delight as she runs into a lawn sprinkler, golden curls bouncing around an angelic face, small chubby hands grasping the hem of her dress. Another, an artistic wedding photo, newlyweds in a romantic embrace, bride glancing over her shoulder with a moody expression and overdone "smokey eyes". It reminded Anna of an eighties music video. Various happy memories were emblazoned on the wall in a neat and effective gallery of time. Several pictures depicted two young girls, teenagers, young women, they were clearly sisters, having enough similarities to attest that they were cast from the same mould. The girls appeared close.

"What do you need to talk to me about, do you know where she is, have you found her?" At the same time condescending and imploring Laura addressed her visitor. "No Laura, is ok to call you Laura?" a nod "we haven't found her. I'm currently involved in a case that may have some connections. I can't go into details but when I was checking out the case history there was a male involved that seems to have had links with your sister. Have you heard from her since she moved away? I can see that you were very close," hand and eyes flicked towards the photo wall "I would imagine that you would be the first person to talk to if she was about to make a life changing decision like moving out of the area?"

"She hasn't moved away!" Laura snapped out the words and turned away from Anna, raising a hand to her mouth, to prevent any further breach of etiquette it would seem. Eyes glistening, brimming with threatening tears. Laura swiped at her eyes, removing any trace of weakness, she shuffled in her seat, pulling her skirt down over her knees, struggling for composure. "Laura, it's OK." Anna's voice was gentle, soothing, despite the woman's brusque manner it was easy to understand why she had developed it. "I can't imagine the situation you're in, not having contact with a loved one for so long, your sister. It must be incredibly distressing, not knowing where she is. I can't say I'm going to help because I don't know if I can. I just know I need to find out more information about the man that I referred to. Perhaps he has some information about where she moved to?" A pause, allowing the words to sink in, Laura had composed herself sufficiently and was now fixedly starring at Anna, as cool as a cucumber. "What did you mean when you said she didn't move away?" "She disappeared. She wouldn't have just moved away like that. Her boyfriend told me that she had moved on, that they had split up and she couldn't handle it, that Social Services were hounding her and she had to get herself and her daughter out of the way, to start again." A flash of blame directed squarely at Anna "I believed him at first. She had a few...issues. But she was getting back on track. We all supported her, my mum and dad, I certainly did, we loved her and Emily of course, that sweet little girl." Laura looked towards the art exhibition, tears welling up in her eyes, she blinked and a solitary tear traced a pattern around the arch of her cheek, coming to a halt at the corner of her mouth. Laura brushed it away. "Who was her boyfriend Laura?" "I didn't really know him, she kept him away from the family, I think she was a little embarrassed by him. He was called Dave though, I remember that. He seemed nice enough, quite good looking. The thing is, Karen had two lives. She was brought up in a good, honest, respectable family. She did well at school, she went to University, was a really bright girl" Laura said this with such earnestness it made Anna feel uncomfortable. "Laura, none of us are perfect, and I'm sure we've all done things to be ashamed of. I can see that Karen had a lot going for her, what happened?" Satisfied that Anna had understood that Karen had some value, some positive attributes that made her worthy of discussion, of hope, she continued "She fell in with the wrong crowd at Uni. I'm not sure what she was taking but she was on some kind of drugs. She ended up coming home and telling us that she was pregnant, she was keeping the baby and she wasn't going back to finish her degree. She was...different. Well, I'm saying different, it was subtle, I think she was depressed. But she wouldn't talk to me about it, she seemed to lose her motivation. Even when Emily came along, she loved her, don't get me wrong, but she always seemed a bit awkward around her, as if she didn't know how to behave with her, I don't know. It was strange, like she was in a dream" "Did she go to the GP's? Get any help?" "No, she wouldn't, we tried to get her to go, I think we felt, as a family, we could get her through whatever she was going through. She eventually met this man, Dave, and she seemed to get a little life back, but it was only brief. As I said, she didn't really discuss him. She struggled to open up" "How did your parents take this, it must have been difficult for them?" "Of course it was, they were devastated when they found out she was pregnant. They had high hopes for Karen, had invested a lot into her education. That is not to say they wouldn't support her though. They would give her money when she needed it and made sure that Emily was provided for. It wasn't ever the same between them afterwards though. I had the feeling that Karen felt they didn't love her, they were just doing their duty." "And did they, love her?" Laura paused a second, glancing again to the wall of memories "Their relationship with her changed, but yes, I think they did." Anna was internally deflated. She could see a young woman who hadn't lived up to the expectations of her family, from either having some kind of mental ill health, dabbling in drugs or both and had took off, daughter in tow, to get away from their weighty disappointment.

It was simple, no mystery here and obviously why any authority who may have investigated it at the time would have ceased to dig any further. "What do you know about Dave? I know you've told me that Karen didn't involve you too much in her life but what can you remember about him?" Laura was pulled from a private reverie "Erm, as I said, he seemed to be quite nice. I believe he had travelled around, he seemed to take to Emily, Karen said he was always spoiling her. He was quite good looking. That's about it, I didn't see him that many times, perhaps he was at Karen's house when I called around to see her. He didn't come to either mine or my parent's house. She didn't involve him in any family get-togethers." "Do you know where he lived?" "I'm afraid not, the last time I saw him was in town, it was shortly after Karen had gone missing. I happened to see him while I was shopping. It's then he told me that she had moved away." "Did Karen never tell you where he lived, anything about him at all?" It was beginning to dawn on Laura that Dave, her sister's old boyfriend was an important piece of the puzzle. "Has he got something to do with her disappearance?" "Laura, we're not sure yet that she did disappear. I wanted to speak with him as he was the last person to have any information. Karen may well be in need of some support and if the social services department of the area that she is now living in doesn't know about her then she won't be able to get that support. I know that you're aware that she had a Social Worker. She was struggling to care for Emily, to keep her safe. Karen may not have told you about the support that she was receiving from us but I can tell you that it was significant. Dave was the last known contact that we have for Karen, he might be the key to finding out where she is so that I can pass this information on. Why are you so sure she didn't just want to make a fresh start, why do you think she has disappeared?" Laura fidgeted in her seat, no longer comfortable with the conversation. "She was my sister" the arrogant tone, and half sneer returning to her face. Maybe it was the mention of social services involvement casting a stain on an upstanding, reputable family. "Of course I know that she wouldn't just leave and not get in touch with us. I spoke to her at least weekly, visited her every couple of weeks. The children played together, she was still involved with the family. My parents might not have been happy with her choices but they didn't exclude her. She wouldn't have just moved away like that, she needed us, Emily needed us." "Is there anything at all Laura, please, think carefully. Laura raised her hand to her forehead, rubbing temples between thumb and middle finger. "There was one occasion, and I'm not sure if she was seeing Dave at this point so there may be no connection at all. Emily was staying with us for the weekend to give Karen a break. She asked me to drop her off at Kennel Bank Road. The only reason I remember this is because it's not a particularly nice area. She told me she was visiting a friend, a potential boyfriend, she laughed when she told me this, I think she knew it would annoy me." "Did you see which house she went into?" "No, she didn't, she waved us off from the pavement exactly where I had left her, she didn't move until I was out of sight. Emily was in the back of the car, she didn't stop waving until we were half way home!" Laura laughed a half laugh, saddened by the fact that she no longer had any contact with her family, a poignant scene that would be eternally etched in her memory. Despite Laura's demeanour towards Anna she felt pity for her. This woman was battling her demons, she clearly loved her sister and her niece, she missed them, had thoughts of what could have been, family barbecues, weddings, a myriad of memorable photo opportunities to adorn the back wall. Anna could imagine that the not knowing would gnaw away at Laura's mind like an insatiable worm, perhaps causing this somewhat caustic exterior to protect itself from the potential horrors that might have befallen her loved ones. "Laura, I'm going to leave my number and if you remember anything else I want you to call me, OK? If I find out anything about Karen's whereabouts, if I get consent from her, I'll be in touch." Laura looked up at Anna who was now standing, ready to leave. "If you get consent?" Incredulous, bitter words. "Yes, maybe she doesn't want to be found." Anna had to take into account the possibility that Karen was out there, living a life separate from her family, devoid of the constant disapproval she could see in her parent's eyes. A life without condemnation. And if she were to be found, she may well not want a reunion, she had to be honest with Laura. Anna's role was bound by confidentiality, as excruciating as that could be at times, she accepted it as part of her job and suffered the consequences. "I have to go out now, erm, Helen? If you hear anything, and you are allowed to pass it on, please feel free to end my misery." She was not impressed, sarcasm cut through her voice like a sharpened razor blade. The discussion was over, but Anna felt that she had made some headway. "Thank you for your time Laura" she had just about enough time to utter the words as the door was unceremoniously slammed behind her.

Chapter Eighteen

"Hey Julie, how are you?" Did that sound disingenuous? Charlie hoped that his waning empathy was sufficiently masked. "I've come for a chat. Obviously everyone is concerned about what happened to Whitney, I thought we could have a bit of a discussion about it." Charlie glanced at the officer that was stood behind him, hoping to convey an air of nonchalance and disdain that she would identify with. A case of I want to talk to you but had to bring this idiot with me. Julie understood his cue, widening her eyes slightly at the officer and motioning for Charlie to enter her flat. He acquiesced, bowing his head slightly as he moved into her territory, not withdrawing his gaze unless allowed to do so by her.

They entered the living room which appeared to have gathered a substantial amount of dirt since his last visit. Charlie gave this no attention, focusing on Julie and allowing her to control the players in her drama. He would allow her to take the lead, to have some control, hopefully this would be a technique that would allow him to ascertain what had happened to her daughter, at least in some part. "Can I sit down, Julie?" "Course you can, Charlie innit? I remember you, how's that slag of a social worker that took mi kid?" Charlie sat on the grimy sofa, trying to perch so as to have minimal contact with it. Julie sat in front of him on a small coffee table that he doubted would take her weight for very long. The officer intuitively stood behind Julie, out of sight, allowing her the perception of freedom to talk. Ignoring the last comment Charlie leaned forward "The police are struggling to find any information about what happened to Whitney." "That's cos their fucking useless." She took a packet of cigarettes from the pocket of marl grey jogging pants, she rummaged in the packet which appeared empty and produced a half smoked cigarette. "Do you know what happened to her, what I mean is, have the police told you about her injuries?" Her bravado diminishing just a little as she delved into her other pocket for a lighter, she struggled to form a flame with it, thumb snapping over the cog in gradually more aggressive attempts. Charlie reached over and took the lighter from her hand, he was more successful in his attempt and lit her cigarette. She took a long drag and looked away, was it contempt, shame, he found it difficult to read, perhaps a mixture of both. "Julie?" "Yeah, I know what they told me anyway, doesn't mean to say they're telling the truth does it?" "Why would they lie?" Julie snorted, her disbelief punctuated by a loud, pretentious belly laugh. "Cos they're pigs! They don't need a fucking reason!" This wasn't going the way he had planned, "Julie, when I met you before it was pretty clear to me that you love your daughter, I can't imagine that you would knowingly allow someone to hurt her like this. Sometimes, for lots of different reasons, people get duped. Someone will come along, say all of the right things and get you to trust them. It happens to us all Julie, in one way or another, it's just being human, do you know what I mean?" Julie starred at him, saying nothing, showing less. "I'm going to say something now that you're not going to like, but I'm going to say it anyway" Charlie's voice was calm and non-judgemental, attempting to coax Julie into a space where she was able to give up her secrets. "I think you might know more than you're letting on" She started to protest but Charlie hushed her, "No, listen to me. I'm not saying you knew what was happening to Whitney, what I'm saying is that I think that maybe you're trying to protect someone that had access to her. Are you scared? Is that the problem?" Her demeanour changed, suddenly broken, lost, but only for a second, a blink and Charlie would have missed it, "I'm not scared of anyone" The bravado was back, this was turning into a much more complicated dance than Charlie had anticipated. He decided to change tack again "What support are you getting at the moment Julie, do you have friends that you can talk to about what's going on?" She shrugged, at once non-committal and self-pitying. "It's easy to get lost in these situations, would you like me to refer you for an advocate, something like that? It's always better to talk things through with someone, you know?" "Yeah, why not" a quiet laugh into her hand that was covering her mouth. "I've had a pretty shit life, yer know" Charlie didn't speak, his eyes conveyed to her that he was willing to hear her story. "When I had Whitney I wanted things to change, wanted to be a bit "normal", do you know what I mean?" Charlie nodded. "But, her dad fucked off and I ended up with a council flat and a kid, ah, whatever eh? That's fucking life." A long, drawn out sigh, Julie summarising the fruits of her adult life. "Dave." She spat out the word as though it was venom she had just sucked from the bite of an angry viper. "Dave who, Julie?" "I dunno if I know his last fucking name, can you believe that?" She laughed to herself. Perhaps a dawning realisation of her circumstance. "Tell me about Dave" Behind Julie the officer had taken out a notepad, fortunately she seemed oblivious, caught up in her own reveries.

* * *

Julie contemplated what she was about to tell Charlie. She hoped her act was drawing them in, she was fully aware that her actions and words would be used later. It seemed to be working, this idiot in front of her, with his kind and gentle ways, what a prick, she surmised he hadn't been in the job for too long, was hell bent on finding her inner humanity. It was worth a try, he appeared to be swallowing the bullshit she was feeding him. At any rate, she was beginning to believe that she could pin the whole thing on Dave, He had done it for fuck's sake, not her. It was her kid, she didn't realise he was gonna get so heavy with her. He did these things and then left her to deal with the pigs and baby snatchers. That bastard needed bringing down a peg or two. How dare he just fuck her off for that skinny bitch he was now shacked up with? She wasn't so stupid to believe his lies. He wasn't with the skank to protect her, Julie, he was sorting himself out and leaving her to deal with the repercussions. A mental image of Dave with the woman was conjured up in her bitter mind, it wasn't the first. The last couple of days had been a tortuous path of betrayal. She saw them laughing together, kissing, having sex, taking the piss out of her. She couldn't allow this to happen. If Dave wasn't going to stand by her through this she had to make sure he didn't find comfort in the arms of another woman. Fuck the consequences for herself, as long as he got what he deserved she didn't care. She weighed up what the police were likely to believe that would leave her in the least amount of shit. She decided she could get away with it, conscious of the officer stood behind her, no doubt with his trusty note book in hand she leaned forward to Charlie. "I met Dave at the club when I was out with the girls, he seemed nice enough, I'm not so sure now though" Julie looked down into her lap, an expression of self-pity spreading across her ample features. "Why do you say that Julie?" "We started to see each other, and he seemed Ok yer know? Then when he met my Whitney he told me he was starting up as a photographer and wanted to take some pics for his port... erm" "Portfolio?" Charlie suggested, Julie nodded, "Yeah, somert like that, he took some really lovely photos of her an'all" Julie motioned to a small photograph on a drab wall in the corner of the room. The photo depicted Whitney, dewy eyed, starring into the soul of the observer, the child did not look happy, quite the opposite, Charlie realised that the image starring back at him, innocent and scared, would haunt him in his dreams for some time to come. "Ok..?" "He told me she could be a child model, he just needed to get some more professional shots, yer know, better lighting and all that stuff. He took her to his studio." "Did you go to this studio with him?" Was that too much information, should she tell them that she had been to his flat? Deciding not "No, I didn't go, but yer know, I'd bin with him for a while then, I trusted him. D'yer think it were 'im, seriously?" She erupted into an emotional outburst with dry eyes, body wracking with incongruous torment. This did not go unnoticed by either the police officer, who had seen it all before, or Charlie, who was learning more about human nature than he would care to. The officer decided to intervene. "Ms Clayton, I think we might need to go down to the station to get a little bit more information. I know this is a difficult time for you but if we are going to find the person responsible for the injuries sustained to your daughter we need a statement from you." Julie looked at the PO, she hoped she was making the right impression, that of an outraged mother, a victim, an innocent party. "Yeah, course I will."

Chapter Nineteen

Dave slid the key into the Yale lock on the front door of the flat. The lack gave with a resistive creak and he entered the hall. With the exception of an angular wedge of sunlight, offered entry by the open door, the hallway was perfectly dark. Closing the door behind him Dave breathed a slow, noisy exhale. He enjoyed entering this place, it gave him a sense of satisfaction, relief, enjoyment and he liked to savour each time he set foot in the place. It was his shrine, altar and sanctuary. A place where he could truly be himself, indulge his desires and recall the ghosts of the past to his present in glorious and vivid detail. He often found himself drifting off, had since he was a child. The ambient noises around him would quiet, his eyes would melt into a stare, focussing on events that those around him could not perceive, undoubtedly something would break through into his waking dream, a blaring car horn, a dog's bark, child's cry. He preferred to indulge in a place of safety, and this, his flat, was it.

The flat was small, from the narrow hallway there were three doors, one led to a living come kitchen area, another to the bathroom and the third an erstwhile bedroom, now referred to as the Studio of Dreams. Dave walked slowly to the door, a lascivious grin forming on his lips as if he was approaching a lover. He stood in front of the door and raised a hand to it, tracing a snake form down the roughly painted central panel with his middle finger. Turning, he entered the living area, flicking on a light he glanced around the room, a nod of approval he made his way to the kitchenette, retrieving a bottle of Jack Daniels from the counter. Sitting down on a worn, tan leather sofa he gulped from the bottle, then allowed a measured breath to escape he lungs. Dave liked to think of himself as an intellectual, not in terms of having a wall full of degree certificates but of having the understanding of how the world works. A way that others could not, or did not have the insight to understand. He believed himself to be a master manipulator, of understanding weakness as a lion would pick off a weak, young or injured member of the herd. Lions fascinated him, and he saw himself as somewhat a kindred spirit, they thought nothing of rape and the slaughter of young. The world for a lion was black and white, kill or be killed, and in a very basic form this was how Dave viewed the world. He perceived his fellow humans as fair game, to be bent, in one way or another, to his will, to fulfil some need that he had. Men, women or children, they were all the same. Inferior bit part players in his drama. He sighed and rubbed a hand absent mindedly against the arm of the sofa, it was quiet in the flat, the road was off the beaten track so even an odd car was an unusual occurrence. He enjoyed it, it allowed him to quiet his mind, maintain some focus. He sometimes felt that his head contained the organic equivalent of white noise, so many thoughts, images and sounds seemed to rush through his head, he found it difficult to concentrate, to maintain some semblance of normality. It wasn't all of the time, perhaps when he was at his neediest, when he was due a fix. One corner of Dave's mouth turned upward in a gross imitation of a smile. He remembered, when young that he was afraid these thoughts, had been convinced that others may see what lay behind his solemn face. How could this turmoil inside his head not go unnoticed? He had visualised that in place of a brain he had a vicious soup of tar, thick and black and ready to burst out of his ears if he did not garner all of his concentration to keep it contained within his skull. Once or twice he had literally put his fingers in his ears to prevent the black matter from escaping, from showing the world what he truly was. As he had grown, he had realised this was a childish fantasy, no one was capable of uncovering the secrets within his mind, and he was more than capable of switching on a personality to suit the situation, the person he wanted to befriend. In addition to Dave's cruel obsessions he also had a fascination with films. He would study the characters, not suspending his belief for one moment, rather studying the actors ability or otherwise to portray genuine emotion and personality. It was an obsession that had faired him well, he felt he had learned many things, the subtle nuances of a conversation, congruent body language, creating a fantasy character that so many had found irresistible. The sweetest part of the whole charade was to then reveal his true self, remove the mask, lift the fog. Got them every time. It was a strange path he had taken in life, one very few others, if anyone would ever understand. Far from feeling alienated by this, he revelled in it, it made him feel superior, an X man, mutant gene forging the way in terms of human evolution. He did often wonder, however, why him, had he been chosen by some unseen force, or was the genetic stride forward a result of his unorthodox upbringing? His father, now there was a man with a mission, a figure to look up to that Dave had found impossible to replace by others. His father had taught him how to survive in this world, a world full of fakes and inferiors. He remembered fondly an exchange. "Right son, this is what mi Dad told me and it's what I'm gonna tell you, yeah?" Dave could see his father's face in front of him, slicked back black hair and a glint in his blue eyes, a rough handsomeness that would be favoured in a Jane Austin novel and a trait Dave had inherited. "Women are only good for two things, the house and bed, do yer get me son?" It wasn't a question that required an answer, this was a mantra that was chanted to the boy Dave on many an occasion. Like a teenager looking for the meaning of life with a fringe religion Dave listened to the mantra, consumed it, made it his own. Only Dave believed he had surpassed his father's delicious yet raw beliefs. He didn't overpower his victims with fear, not initially, he used a much more sophisticated technique. He used their minds, their guilt, their addictions, obsessions, innocence. The mantra played on in Dave's head "Women will cause you nothing but strife son, yer 'av to put 'em in their place, tame em. If yer don't, they'll be sneaking off like 'ungry dogs looking for their next bit 'o meat. And they need proper training lad, not just a slap 'ere and there." Dave had understood this, even as a child, he was aware that men and women were very different, had noticed the interactions, consequences, statuses were poles apart. He had been a willing student of his father's teachings, he had only contempt for his mother and sister, had seen the way they pathetically attempted to use their weaknesses against him and his father. The soft voices, trying to lull them, strip them of their machismo, tears, screams. It had no effect, he had learned from his father that these were ways to emasculate, to gain power over him and he wasn't prepared to relinquish his power, not for his mother, his sister, no inferior bitch would ever be able to tame him. A vision of his mother, superimposed onto the equally worn sofa that was positioned opposite. Black blood against white sheets in a room lit by a street lamp. Her white body quivering, the screams and protests and pleas had long since diminished, now a guttural, interrupted breath, akin to an emphysema sufferer, eyes darting from father to son, then glazing over, a final exhale, a fixed stare straight ahead appearing to question the third drawer of the dressing table immediately adjacent to her eye line. Then nothing, a calm that consumed him, caused excitement, an exhilaration he had never experienced before. His father caught his eye, for a moment he had completely forgotten that he was even in the room. He looked at him "Dad?" He was overwhelmed, he had never experienced such power over another human being, such control. He could manipulate their life or death, beginning and end, it was a revelation that was the closest thing to spiritual he had ever experienced. His young mind had accepted this without question, without the grandiosity of intellectualism, just a basic, feral right to power over human life. And as a child he enjoyed it, became aroused by it, would ruminate over every detail, every trickle of blood, every wail, it fulfilled him, made him feel like a man, an equal to his father.

* * *

Dave sighed, the memory of the dead woman played upon his face like an old man's reverie of a long gone, beloved girlfriend. Dave abruptly stood and made his way to the bedroom door, again he stroked the door, a body to be caressed and cajoled into untold pleasures. Dave slid his hand seductively to the handle and depressed it, opening the door widely, allowing some filtered light to spill into the room. The harsh glow revealed a wedge of a bed, clean white sheet covering the surface, the corner of the room was also visible, a tripod stand with a light, unlit, and an umbrella behind, a quadrant of grey old walls, a portion of a teddy bear, mid-section upwards, lying at an angle to the pillow it had been propped upon laying on the bed like an unsuspecting protagonist in a fairy tale. Dave's eyes wandered across the tableau, his chest filling with air, attempting to draw in the whole room, absorb the deeds that had been committed here, pull in the memories of acts that had provided him with some kind of relief, satisfaction. He had spent a long time perfecting the room, soundproofing the walls, floor and ceiling with two inch thick boards. He had then painstakingly erected further insulation behind a stud wall just to be entirely sure. He had finished the room in stark white matt emulsion, now a dull grey in the dim light, he believed this would give a better quality contrast and finish to his films. The project had taken him around three months in all, sourcing the correct materials, obsessing over the finishing touches, a real labour of love. He flicked on a light switch and a garish fluorescence assaulted the room. Aside from the bed and lighting equipment there was little more in here. A tripod stand at the foot of the bed with a digital camcorder attached to it, eye starring fixedly at the white sheet. A box of toys, props, was placed neatly in the far corner of the room.

A Barbie doll's arm lay over the side of the box as if attempting to make an escape. In the fluorescent lighting the room was now a stark white, not grey. A small clothes rail held a variety of dressing up costumes, small costumes, fairies, princesses, cowgirl, a box of accessories lay neatly beneath, a glittering wand, star atop poked magically out of the box. Despite the colourful array of toys and clothing the room had a clinical appearance, a doctor's examination room. Dave was stock still, gazing at the bed that dominated the room, his eyes beginning to roll upward into his head. Hand moving down to the zip of his trousers he let out a throaty, depraved breath, his body began to spasm unable to control the pleasures that he had taken from innocents in this room and the sweet anticipation of those to come, soon. Dave knew that this moment in time, the delicious build up, the thrill of the chase was almost as good as the final act. He had visited the room many times over the past few days, exercising this ritual of longing, fantasising, plotting, planning. When finished, he walked over to the bed, picking up the teddy bear and straightening it out on the pillow, he smiled a cruel smile at the bear, the bear, with glassy, brown eyes, looked on.

Chapter Twenty

Charlie tried for the third time to connect to Anna on the phone and for the third time he was connected to the answer machine. He had left messages each time, and each one becoming progressively more urgent. Where was she? She had told him in the earlier phone conversation that she was going to speak with a contact from an old case, and that she may know the whereabouts of "Dave". She had also told him that she would email him details of the information she had found out so far, just to keep him up to speed. It wasn't like Anna to not answer her phone. She was aware that calls from colleagues would usually be urgent. Health and Safety policies were rammed down the work forces neck and the lone working policy was paramount. Workers had to detail their every move on their online calendars, the team whiteboard and log their activities with the fierce admin workers. It was a pain in the arse but had to be adhered to, and Anna was no exception. More than once she had fallen foul of the office manager and had learned to toe the line. Charlie had checked Anna's calendar before leaving the office, the whole day was mapped out as "working from home". He needed to get back to the office to check his emails, maybe that would give him a clue as to where she was, a growing unease began to claw it's way into his mind and his belly, something just wasn't right. He subconsciously held his breath as he descended the urine soaked stairwell and left the depressing complex of flats, breaking in a run as he neared his car.

Chapter Twenty-one

Laura sat before him fidgeting and wringing her hands, like a coiled spring ready to unleash it's pent up anguish on the world. It had been a long drive, the sun in his eyes had caused a headache to brew at his temples. He felt uncomfortable, as if his clothes were attempting to asphyxiate him, skin itched under the weight of his skirt and jacket. "Thank you for seeing us at such short notice Laura. I'm Detective Inspector Cooper and this is my colleague PC Crawshaw." A nod, the DI could almost taste her impatience. "There is no easy way to say this Laura, we've found two bodies who we believe may be your sister and your niece" He paused, allowing the words to sink in. PC Crawshaw, a keen young female officer with far too much ambition and very little empathy jumped in "We have some remnants of clothing that we need you to iden..." "Laura, these last few years must have been absolute hell, the not knowing. I can't imagine what it's been like for you?" The DI cut in, affording the young PO a disapproving glance, she sat back on the sofa, he was sure he caught a look of indignation flash across her face. He would deal with that later, right now he was breaking the most difficult news to a family member and he couldn't be pulled off track. "Laura, I know this is going to be difficult, time has passed but I'm going to have to ask you to remember any detail that you can think of around the time that Karen disappeared." The woman, who had initially been quite brusque, had had the wind knocked out of her sails. He immediately felt overwhelming sympathy for her. "Have you spoken to the Social Worker?" The DI was a little thrown by the comment. "Erm, no, which Social Worker would this be?" "She was here this morning, asking me questions about Karen, asking about her boyfriend, Dave. Did he have something to do with this?" "Do you have the name of the worker Laura?" The DI glanced at the PO and nodded to her, indicating that she needed to make notes, the officer snapped her pad open, biro poised over the blank sheet, she didn't look at her superior, rather, her eyes were fixed on Laura. This woman really needs to work on her interpersonal skills, he thought. "It was Anna Dawson, she seemed quite interested in Dave, she told me she was working with another family and she needed to speak with him regarding something, well, something to do with the family I presume." "Well, thank you for that, we'll get hold of Ms Dawson later. Now, is there anything that you can remember about the day that Karen and Emily went missing?" Laura proceeded to relate the details she had given to Anna the previous day, with one or two more insights. She had barely slept last night, Anna's visit reopening old wounds, not that they had ever really healed, just formed a fragile scab, a scab that would rub off at the mere mention of a name, a child's laugh. "Do you remember what Karen and Emily were wearing when they went missing?" "Yes, I do, I had seen them both in the morning, we were going to shop for Emily's birthday present but Karen had called it off, she told me she had something else to do so she wanted to meet up the following day. It was raining and when I arrived at their house Emily had a little pink Mac and some pink wellington's I had bought for her a week or two ago, she looked so sweet..." Laura drew in a lengthy breath, this was difficult for her and the DI knew it, but he needed to get this information before she viewed the clothing. Experience told him that exposure to the physical evidence of the death of a loved one could have devastating results. She would be unlikely to be in a position to talk to him, it was vital he got the information he needed first. "So, Karen's boyfriend, David Cartwright, do you know where he is now?" "No, as I said, I never went to his house, I had dropped Karen off at Kennel Bank Road at some point around the time that she may have been seeing him but I couldn't say that he lived there. I'm sorry, I feel useless." Laura's shoulder's hunched forward, hands covered her face. "Laura, do you want to call your husband, it's probably best not to be alone right now. We have some clothing that we would like you to identify. We can get someone to pick you up and bring you over to the station when you're ready, ok?" "What happened to them, you haven't told me?" It was a straight forward question that the DI didn't have such a straight forward answer to. "We don't know yet Laura, they were found together, in a shallow grave. Now this is going to be hard but I'd rather you hear it from me than read about it in the paper ok?" She nodded, it was half hearted, part of her wanted to know all of the grisly details, and part of her wanted to remain oblivious, pretend that her sister and her niece were out there somewhere, alive. "We suspect foul play, the remains were found together in a wood in Greater Manchester. A woman was out walking her dog and the dog unearthed some of the remains. We aren't sure how they passed but the pathologist will hopefully give us something to go on." The DI's voice was calm and practical, he as yet had not determined a way to break this kind of news to families that sheltered them from harsh reality. He had learned, by experience, that in hind sight they had been grateful of the truth. "Did they...suffer?" Her voice broke on the last word, he realised silent tears were streaming down her face. "Laura, I want to tell you no, god knows I do. But the truth is we just don't know what happened yet. When we find out, I promise you this, you'll be the first to know. Now, where is your husband, I want you to give him a call and ask him to come home. Officer Crawshaw here will stay with you until he gets here." Outside of the house DI Cooper surveyed the idyllic semi-rural panorama before him, a stark contrast to the sickening acts that had been committed against Laura's loved ones. The DI often contemplated the polarities that this world had to offer and after many years in the service had not been able to draw any logical conclusions. The world and the humans that inhabited it simply were what they were, there was no point attempting to draw sense from it. DI Cooper called his office, he needed the number of the Social Worker looking into this case, it was likely she had made some connections and he needed to let her know that they were investigating more than a missing person.

Chapter Twenty-two

Charlie switched on his PC and utilised the time it took to load up to speak with the admin workers. He determined that Anna had not called in to state she was going on any visits, at least she hadn't called in. Charlie knew from earlier conversations that she was planning to speak with relatives of the historical case. The admin did tell him that a DI Cooper had left several messages for her in connection with a case. Following a quick detour to make a strong coffee Charlie seated himself at his desk, PC not yet loaded he checked his phone, no missed calls, no texts. What the hell was she playing at! He attempted to calm himself down, maybe she had decided to take some flexi, he was aware that she had accrued more hours that she would be allowed to take as leave. But if that was the case that is exactly what it would say on her calendar, and it didn't. She was "working from home". Finally, the PC came to life, allowing him a portal to a plethora of broken lives, and Outlook. He double clicked the mail icon, the egg timer whizzed around for what seemed to take an age. Ah! A message from Anna, almost three hours ago, he skimmed the message, taking in bits of information and then forced himself to slow down. She was going to visit the relative of an old child protection case that had been stacked, client possibly moved out of area, believing that David Cartwright was somehow involved with the case. It was the same case that the DI had been calling about. He walked back down to the admin desk "Have you got a contact number for the DI that was trying to get a?" "I've sent her a phone message email, it's on there"

.n woman, Tina, was a fine student of her line manager, she

.ed in exuding disdain on any question asked of her. "Anyway,

. on my break" She turned away with a whip of blond hair that was tied in a high ponytail atop her teak complexioned face. Charlie leaned over her desk to impress what he was about to say "I need that number, this is incredibly important, now if you value your job, such as it is, I suggest you find that number for me and bring it over to my desk within the next thirty seconds" Charlie's voice remained calm during the exchange but the seething frustration was more than evident. Tina starred at him for a second, her mouth forming a perfect "o" resembling a blow up doll, the memory of this would cause him to chuckle in months to come, right now it was making his blood boil. He turned on his heels and returned to his desk, a few workers attempting to engage him in questioning glances, he ignored them. Tina composed herself, drawing in as much dignity as she could following this assault and proceeded to tap away at her PC, her scarlet coloured nail extensions reminiscent of the pecking beaks of exotic birds, she then scribbled down a telephone number and reluctantly walked across the office to place the post it note, silently, on Charlie's desk.

“Thank you" Phone already in hand Charlie called the mobile number scribbled on the yellow paper. A click and a clipped voice "Hello, DI Cooper?" "Hello, Detective Inspector, this is Charlie Archer from Kirklees Social Services, I understand that you have been trying to contact my colleague, Anna Black?" "Yes, yes, that's right. I wanted to speak with her in connection with a case that I'm working on. Do you know how I can get hold of her?" "This is the thing, I'm aware that she has been looking into an old case today, a woman and child that went missing some time ago Karen and Emily Osborne?" Nothing, no response, he continued. "She went out to speak with Laura Cassidy sister of Karen Osborne and I haven't been able to get hold of her all day. I was going to call Laura to gather a bit more information. Anna believes that David Cartwright, who I'm sure you're aware of, has something to do with a case that Anna is working on. He was also involved with Laura's sister. I decided to call you just in case you had any more information? This may sound a little histrionic but I'm becoming quite concerned. Anna isn't the sort of person to go out on calls and not report back. Apart from a call earlier, I've heard nothing and neither has anyone else in the office." "Have you tried her home phone, personal emails, personal mobile?" "Yes, everything, and no joy" "It seems that she may be looking for Mr Cartwright. The address that we have on file is his parents address in Rochdale, we have an officer en route to see if he actually lives there. What can you tell me about Dog Kennel bank?" "Erm, well it accommodates a fair few transient individuals, a few students, not the most salubrious area in Huddersfield, why?" "Karen's sister mentioned it to me. Would you like to meet me there?" Charlie's concern was growing by the minute, what had Anna got herself mixed up in? "Of course, when?" "As soon as you can" the line clicked, dead. Charlie stared at the handset for a few seconds, he felt a snake like churning in the pit of his stomach, something was seriously wrong. His PC had just about loaded up and he decided to check his emails one more time before leaving the office. Thirty four unread, one from Anna "Just to let you know that I'm going to have a look around Dog Kennel Bank, it's possible Dave lives around there somewhere, could you put it on the board for me, Ta." A tagline..."Sent from my Iphone4" She had sent the email from her personal phone at eleven forty seven, it was now three. He had spoken with her at about half ten when she had asked him to help the police officer speak with Julie. He had left the office at around eleven forty five to meet with the officer at Julie's flat, two minutes! If anything had happened to her he would never forgive himself. Breaching protocol he left the office, he didn't write his expected whereabouts on the white board and he didn't inform his manager, she wasn't at her desk and tracking her down, then explaining the situation would waste valuable time. Charlie barged though the exit door, ignored the frequently broken down lift and took the stairs two at a time.

Chapter Twenty-three

Anna walked through the doorway, each step taking what seemed like minutes. Her senses were in overdrive, she knew that this was not within her jurisdiction but the panic that had been swelling within her belly drove her forward. The flat had an odour that she had not expected, rather than the aroma of male sweat and dirty dishes that she would have associated with a flat belonging to Dave the acrid aroma of bleach assaulted her senses. Aside from the morning sun behind her there was little light in the hallway, she reached around and closed the door noting where the light switch was. Anna suddenly realised she wasn't breathing. Leaning against the backdoor she forced herself to take a breath and get a hold of herself. She knew the flat was empty, or at least he wasn't here. She had to find out was happening, the police were taking their time and she was concerned another child might be at risk. This in mind she also told herself that she didn't want to be front page news as a Social Worker that breaks into the houses of men with tenuous links to her clients. Stop! Her internal argument was wasting time, she needed to satisfy herself, but satisfy herself of what exactly? Walk Anna! One foot in front of the other, the nearest door first, she had no way of knowing just how long Dave would be out of the flat, she needed to hurry. Why didn't she bring Charlie with her, because Charlie isn't an idiot and he wouldn't be doing anything so ridiculous? She opened the door, did it really make so much noise or was this in her head? A living room cum kitchen, neat and tidy, no signs of life no other doors, nooks or crannies to explore. She closed the door and moved on, a small bathroom, again neat and tidy, a clean sink held a deodorant can and shaving foam, a small towel was neatly folded on a towel rail. Anna's brow furrowed, had she got the wrong place, this was not the kind of place she would expect of someone who liked to molest children, not in her head anyway. She was seriously beginning to doubt herself when a noise caught her attention, it sounded like a half scrapping, half shuffling sound, coming from the third and final door. Anna's mind suddenly filled with a film she had watched, zombies taking over, lurching after victims and dragging bits of limbs behind them. Don't panic! As she placed her hand on the door handled she struggled to fight back tears, she was in such an anxious state of mind she again had to remind herself why she was there. Her shaking hand depressed the handle, opening the door and pushing it inwards so that she could see the contents of the room. A hand flew to her mouth, stifling a scream. A fluffy, taffeta dress was beside the bed, it was pink and had ruffle upon ruffle of stiff pink netting to puff it out, a little like a ballerina's dress or something that would be worn to an American beauty pageant. It wasn't the dress that horrified Anna, it was the little girl inside it, arms above her head that seemed to be tied to one of the bed's legs, small legs attempting to push against the slippery laminate flooring, there was a puddle of liquid at the child's feet that Anna assumed was urine. A tape across the girl's mouth that had become covered in snot and tears. The girl's eyes noticed Anna and her scrabbling became more frantic. Shocked out of her immobility

Anna rushed over to the girl. The girl's hands were bound with cable ties and had cut through her fragile wrists causing some bleeding, Anna placed her shoulder under the bottom of the bed and pushed upwards, allowing her to slip the girls hands from underneath the bed leg. She then held the little girl, attempting to comfort her while she removed the tape from her mouth. From nowhere, searing, blinding pain at the back of her head, her eyes felt that they had been knocked out of their sockets, disoriented, she was shoved forward with the force of the pain onto her front, the little girl trapped beneath her, all in a split second, then darkness, nothing.

Chapter Twenty-four

Music, a guitar riff, something she had heard before but couldn't quite place. What day was it? Is it morning, the alarm, but she set her alarm to beep. Not the radio, if a nice tune came on it tended to send her back into sleep, had the opposite of the desired effect. Had she been drinking? Her head throbbed and she was struggling to open her eyes, a seductive, familiar voice sang to her but she couldn't place it. Something so familiar in a context that was utterly at odds with her current circumstances. Arms aching, attempting to move, the pain to both her arms and head prevented this. What the hell is happening? An involuntary groan escaped her lips, it sounded muted, far away, she realised her lips hurt and her throat was dry. She needed to get up, have a drink of water and some paracetamol, then determine what had gotten her into this state. She tried to move her arms again, couldn't, why not, numb fingers explored their position, her thumb could feel a slick material against her wrist, was this tape? A sickening wave washed over her, the flat, the little girl, the pain. As realisation dawned she tried very hard not to scream. If he was in the room he would know by now that she was waking up, could she feign unconsciousness until she had time to think? Anna forced her body to go limp, trying to determine if there were any sounds that could give her a clue as to whether or not she was alone. A tune that she had once loved, a classic Jimi Hendrix was playing, it would forever hold an entirely different meaning. She could feel goose bumps rising on her skin, bile crawl it's way up into her throat, burning, making her want to vomit. She attempted to force it back down her throat, a silent swallow that seemed to bellow in her ears. As the reality of her situation took hold Anna's mind seemed to recede into a dream. This cannot be happening, I'm going to wake up any minute. Her senses were overly aroused, light from the room forced itself against her closed eyes, her breath, heartbeat could surely be heard within the room. Anna, come on, you need to get through this, think! Anna's internal dialogue attempted to drag her from the disassociation she was experiencing and force her into action. She had to try and open her eyes but dare not, she was terrified as to what she might see, what horror would be before her. The girl! What about the girl, she was most likely still here. What about the horror that might befall her. Come on Anna, open your eyes. Anna's sense of protection for the vulnerable child overcame her terror, if there was one motivating factor in Anna's life it was protecting the innocent.

A flicker of light, glaring, assaulting her vision, causing splinters of glass sharp pain to add to the tumult that was already present in her head. A little wider, white walls came into focus, fuzzy edges forming sleek white panels. A dark shape silhouetted in front of the stark walls, gaining clarity, focus. Dave. He stood behind a video camera, busily adjusting the settings. He seemed not to notice that she was in front of him, was this some kind of mistake, should she call out to him? "Here she is, my next little starlet, and I must say Anna, one of my more attractive... erm, models." He said this with a flourish, a wave of the hand towards where she lay.

Enjoying the moment, she knew enough about people to recognise that he was getting more than just a cheap thrill from this. He had set this up with a great deal of thought, was quite elaborate and sophisticated in the execution of his plan. He was fulfilling something. There was an intensity in his voice that indicated this was some kind of act? A scene to be played, over and over perhaps? Had this happened to him, as a child, set his morality radar completely off kilter? She noticed a crooked smile spread across his face. Anna turned away, suppressing yet another gag, she scanned the room, now in perfectly normal, but for it, all the more terrifying clarity. The white, clinical walls surrounded her, there were some professional looking lighting equipment to her left, the light on which added to the pain in her head, to the right was a box of toys, the little girl sat beside it in the grotesque party dress. Swollen cheeks had a sheen of dried tears. She was feebly picking toys out of the box and then dropping them back into it, an automaton that had become stuck in a singular process. Every few seconds the child would sob, a bone shaking sob that made her shoulders bounce, she didn't look up at Anna, simply continued to blankly remove each toy from the box and drop it back in.

* * *

"So, you decided to drop by then, Anna? I'm glad you did, I don't often get ladies of your calibre visiting me." The lascivious smile. "Julie's filled me in, she told me that you were responsible for taking away her gorgeous little Whitney, is that right?" It wasn't a question, it was a statement of fact. "No worries, I've been trying to think of a way to get you here, you know? Clearly great minds think alike, you succeeded where it seems I failed. All's well in the world, your here now eh?" An unintelligible sound fell from Anna's lips, she was struggling to form a single thought never mind a response to this utterly bizarre situation. "Well, it's by the by, we have two new little starlets to film, and guess what Anna, your gonna be one of them. I've got something a little special for you though. Have you heard of snuff films, of course you have, what am I saying? A woman of your education, I'm sure you had some little course about it at work, yeah?" Dave stood back on his heels holding one hand to his chest and bowing his head in mock supplication. "An educated woman like you will have all sorts of things in her head, you'll have to forgive me, I'm more adept with junkies and whores. This is going to be a first, for both of us." A wink and the unnerving smile. A second wave of unreality hit her, she felt that she was losing consciousness, the surreal act that was playing out in front of her relegated her mind to believe this was some kind of dream. This couldn't be happening. Why hadn't she taken Charlie's advice and left this to the police? Anna's mind scrabbled for ways to get out of the situation. "Dave, you need to let me and the child go, the police are aware of what's going on, I told them I was coming over here," "Is that right darling? A wry smile "So you told the police you would be breaking and entering into a flat did you?" Dave moved away from the camera, glancing back into the viewfinder, ensuring that the shot was going to be executed to his requirements. "I'll tell you what's going to happen so that it won't be a shock, ok?" The gentleness of the voice was juxtaposed to the words, causing Anna to squirm against the ties that held her to the bed. She was seconds away from total and utter panic, she fought down the need to vomit and desperately racked her brain for some way to gain control over the situation. "So, this is the plan, a double whammy, one that I wasn't expecting, but hey ho, fortune smiles on the brave eh? I'm going to rape you, I'm going to really hurt you, and you're going to scream, don't take it personally, it's what the punters want. Then when I've done you, I'm going to do the little girl. The plan had been to do her and then let her go. Her mother actually agreed to let me do this, can you believe that Anna?" He appeared to be both incredulous and amused by this. "These kids don't really like to talk about what I do to 'em, so my little secret would have been safe, no collateral damage, do you know what I mean? But now that you're in the equation I'll probably have to kill you both, because maybe she will talk, who knows?" "Dave, you have to listen to me" voice quivering with abject terror Anna simultaneously attempted to wriggle her hands free from the tape whilst coming up with something to stall the inevitable. She could feel her bladder begin to relax and had to fight back the tears that this sad, undignified and outrageous situation was reducing her to.

"Before you do what you have to do Dave, please indulge me, why? Why are you doing this, what makes you want to hurt people like this? Forget me, the girl, why would you want to hurt her? If you could tell me, I'd like to know?" Her words sounded fragile in her ears, as if they would shatter before they reached their intended audience. "You really want to know eh Anna? Would it satisfy your curiosity, your middle class, university educated curiosity?" She had said the wrong thing, he was getting angry, a chip on his shoulder, working class roots, intelligence but no conduit to channel it. Anna realised she was panting, she didn't know how much longer she could keep the panic at bay. A tear rolled down the side of her face and caught on the hair above her ear... "I am curious, yes, Dave. Tell me?" "I will tell you Anna, 'cause it won't take long. All of these pathetic attempts to stall me are just not gonna work," He looked down at her, taking in the whole length of her body, then very slowly, back up to her eyes. "Because I like it" He laughed, and Anna knew that short of a miracle she, nor the girl was not going to get out of this situation alive.

Chapter Twenty-five

Charlie pulled onto the corner of Dog Kennel Bank with the intention of walking the length of the road to find DI Cooper. There were no police cars in sight, he determined it must be an unmarked car. He took the path opposite the row of Victorian villas in favour of the path that was adjacent to a pleasant wooded area. Charlie could not help but feel that he would not perceive this vista to be anything but sinister before this day was out. With a heavy heart Charlie made his way along the street, glancing into both cars and houses as he did so, after a minute or so he observed a male, in his thirties leave one of the properties. The male had long hair, tied back in a ponytail, biker gear clad his clearly well-built frame, he glanced up at Charlie with a nod before mounting his motorbike and then made his way down the road. Charlie made a note of the house he had exited and wondered if this could be the guy. Deep in thought he jumped when he felt a hand touch his arm, he spun around to face DI Cooper... "Charlie?" He waited for a response, in this case a nod before continuing. "I'm DI Cooper, could we get into the car and I'll bring you up to date with what we have so far." DI Cooper walked a little further down the road to a black Vauxhall Vectra, he motioned to the back seat and got into the drivers seat. Once in the car Cooper introduced Charlie to his colleague DC Crawshaw, she stared straight ahead without acknowledging Charlie's presence. "Can you tell me anything more than we discussed over the phone Charlie?" DI Cooper asked in a considered tone. Charlie immediately picked up the air of authority exuding from this man, he imagined he was well respected. "Not really, I did receive a brief email from Anna stating that she was going to have a look for this Dave Cartwright, around here, other than that nothing. Can I ask why you're involved, I mean the local CPU are looking into this guy, has he committed offences in your area?" "As yet we are still investigating, but he's our main person of interest at present. The woman and child that your colleague was looking into, Karen and Emily Osborne, their remains have been found in woodland just outside of Rochdale. From what the medical examiner can tell us they were both strangled, there were ligatures found around their necks. Having spoken to a relative, it would seem that Mr Cartwright was one of the last people to see them alive. We need to speak with him as a matter of urgency." Charlie let the information he had just received sink in, it was now possible that this man was, what, a murderer? "We need to find Anna, she said she was coming to look for him, she might be in his house already, what are we waiting for!" Charlie started to get out of the car but the DI placed a hand over his arm. "I know you must be concerned, what we need to do is have a look and see if you can see her car. She may well have gone home. We did a bit of checking up on the flats around here and came across one landlord who could match Mr Cartwright's description but gave us a different name, John James. Said he was the perfect tenant, always paid his rent up front, no issues with neighbours. We think it may be him but we need to be sure." "Ok, Ok, why don't I have a walk up and down the street and see if I can spot Anna's car?" "Fair enough

Charlie, but don't do anything stupid." Getting out of the police car, he scanned the road he had already traversed. Sure he would have spotted Anna's silver 203 but wanting to make absolutely sure. There was no sign of it, he turned and continued up the tree lined path, the road ahead was two, perhaps three hundred yards, he could see a couple of small silver cars but couldn't be sure they were hers. He felt he was being watched, that piercing eyes knew who he was, why he was there. He had a sense that not only he was in danger but that his mere existence on this street was putting Anna at risk. He steeled himself and continued on, he needed to know if she were here, the police needed to know. The first of the cars, a Honda, the second a Peugeot but the wrong model. He could see the rest of the way up the street and there were no more cars fitting Anna's. This couldn't be right, think! Anna wouldn't simply pull up outside the house would she? She would have parked out of sight, around the corner or in a hidden spot. Everyone at the office knew that if they were using their own cars they didn't want them identifying. Many a worker's car had been keyed or some other vandalism inflicted on it by angry parents or disaffected youths. He continued on to the end of the street and noticed some spare ground to the side and set back from the last house. He crossed the road and rounded the corner, there it was, Anna's car. Identifiable by the black and white dangly dice that she refused to get rid of, a gift from her father when she passed her driving test she had once confided, a half smile of pride and slight embarrassment on her face. He had a quick look at the car, nothing remarkable, no broken windows, slashed tires, just an ordinary car.

"Her car's parked up there, around the corner. Where did you say his flat was, or where you think his flat might be?" "Hang on Charlie, I have to say I don't have a particularly good feeling about this, I think we need to call for uniformed officers, just in case. Take a seat and I'll call them now." Charlie reluctantly returned to the car, his frustration evident from his expression and manner. He fidgeted on the back seat, attempting to calm himself but with each passing moment his nerves were fraying, a snap was imminent. He needed distraction, regarding the female DC in the passenger seat of the car Charlie had been vaguely aware that she had failed to speak or interact in anyway during the course of the previous conversation. She appeared quite young, fairly attractive, she swallowed and he noticed that her Adam's apple appeared to bob in her throat. Did women actually have them, perhaps she had some thyroid disorder? Charlie shifted himself in his seat so that he could see her profile more clearly, yes there it was, an apple any man would have been proud of. She swallowed again, Charlie was in awe, the bobbing had a weird grace and beauty about it that transfixed him. A car drove by them and this jerked Charlie out of his bizarre fixation, he suddenly realised he was becoming hysterical. In times of crisis his mind tended to gravitate to the most obscure things. This poor woman's Adam's apple being one fine example. "How long have you been with the police?" He asked DC Crawshaw as much to distract himself from her spell as to see if the woman actually spoke. She turned her head to look at him, an utterly blank expression on her face, with a long slow exhale she turned her head to face the street again. Charlie was almost disturbed by her demeanour. He had had dealings with some pretty frosty police officers but she really topped them all, things were obviously more grim on the other side of the Pennines if this is what the constabularies finest had to offer. DI Cooper had completed his call, "They shouldn't be too long, let's have a wander over, see if we can see what's happening." He spoke to DC Crawshaw, "You stay in the car".

Chapter Twenty-six

Dave looked down at the woman on the bed, she reminded him of his mother, same kind of hair, same tear laden eyes. He despised her. She stood for all of the pathetic weaknesses he abhorred. She had tried to reason with him, pleaded, cried. It was sickening. His dad had the right idea when it came to women, they were as good as mangy dogs that should be put to sleep. That didn't mean to say he couldn't have a bit of fun before they were put out of their inherent feminine misery. Not to mention the money he would make by capturing the moment on film. He knew that the police ruse was just that, a way to buy time, he had heard many desperate ruses from his models, as well as the begging, pleading and crying. A memory came to him, bubbled up to the surface of his brain, he allowed it some space. His sister, nagging his father for a puppy. Her friend was giving them away, an unwanted result of allowing the mutt to roam the streets. After several day of listening to her squawks his father gave in and allowed her to have it. She took the mutt everywhere with her, even to the bathroom. Dave had had a sense that she dare not leave the dog in his vicinity, this both amused and enraged him. He developed a loathing for the thing, a little, fluffy tan cross breed with a face that should have been on an animal shelter advert. An opportune moment arose, he found himself at home early following a flood at his school, his sister was younger and was attending the local primary school, completely oblivious of the devastation he was about to cause her. He had attempted to call the dog, which was loyally waiting on his sister's bed, staring out of her bedroom window, willing her to return. The dog took a brief look at him then returned its gaze to the window. Dave had grabbed the dog by the scruff of the neck, causing it to yowl in pain, the look in its eyes confused. Holding it tightly to his chest Dave took the dog out into the garden, sitting it in a tight space between a dilapidated shed and the garden fence. The dog wagged its tail, head held low in supplication, sad eyes watching him beneath little tufts of tan fur. Dave had looked around the garden, there were various bits of junk to be found. He spotted a large rock and decided that this would do the job, keeping one eye on the puppy Dave retrieved the rock. The puppy, however, had decided it could make it's escape, not fast enough, Dave caught the animal with his foot, stamping on it's hind quarters making escape impossible, the dog whimper and wriggled franticly, turning it's head and frantically biting at Dave's shoe. It was no match. He picked up the dog with his free hand and threw it back into the corner, the dog was now screaming with pain, Dave realised that this may alert his neighbours so he decided to finish the dog off more quickly than he would have liked, bringing the stone down with such a force that it crushed the puppy's skull, splattering blood and brain tissue against the shed and fence. Paws twitched a couple of times and Dave believed he saw the light go out of the sad eyes. He was exhilarated, aroused, alive. Thoughts of tormenting his sister with this act were far from his mind, he had enjoyed the act itself, the dog had been terrified of him, it had seen what he was capable of and feared him. He rushed into the house and raced to the bathroom. Closing the door and resting his back against it, hyperventilating. Forcing himself to settle he regarded his reflection in the bathroom mirror. Speckles of blood flecked his face, his eyes appeared wild. Dave stood like this for several minutes, contemplating his actions, himself and then assimilated the reveries into his psyche, this was who he was. Dave washed his hands and face, picked up his school bag on the way to the door and left the house. He would return at the usual time to find his sister looking for her beloved pet, he smiled.

Back to the present, "Ah Anna, lovely Anna." He grinned at her prone form, could see the cogs grinding inside her head, coming up with nothing, zero, zilch. She wasn't getting out of this. He checked the camera equipment, making sure the device was recording. He debated whether or not to start again, he had no idea how long he had been lost in his reverie, but decided against. The prolonged image of the bound woman, frantic, desperate would no doubt provoke anticipation of what was to unfold. He liked that idea, a piece of art, captured to manipulate the audience's emotions, guide them on a tour of the exquisite. He sat down on the bed at the side of her, her feet scrabbled against the sheets in an attempt to create some distance, her lean back arching as she did so. Her eyes didn't leave him though, wild and terrified. He placed a hand on her belly and felt her wince, sucking in breath to avoid his touch. She appeared shocked by the touch of his flesh on hers, eyes darting over her body, only just realising she was naked. He sniggered, her eyes were back on him, His fingers draped as he slid his hand upwards to cup her breast, a gentle, cold caress. "Please Dave, don't do this" words faltering, she had started to cry, and she had been doing so well. Dave sighed, he had high hopes for this one, she was strong, he believed she would take some breaking, to cry, so soon? Dave rationalised that she perhaps didn't have the narcotic haze to clamber through before realisation of what was happening took hold. None the less, he was very disappointed. Here it was, the guttural, mucus laden sobs started to flow, he felt himself becoming aroused and anger filled him, not yet! Dave snatched his hand away and stood up. "A question for you Anna, do you like dogs?" He didn't give her a chance to respond, his heavy fist connecting with her temple in a split second, knocking her out cold.

Chapter Twenty-seven

Anna was on a beach, it was where she used to go for childhood holidays, some west coast resort she couldn't remember the name of. Surrounding her were wind breakers, a sea of multi coloured, striped shades that protected those inside from the chill breeze that was blown over the Atlantic and into the faces of disappointed holiday makers. Anna glanced around, a sensation of slight unease invading her senses. Despite the numerous deck chairs and wind breakers she couldn't see a solitary soul, the beach was deserted. This wasn't right, the beach should be teeming with people, sad looking donkeys touting for rides, ice cream vendors, signs of life. The ocean had an eerie quality to it, the grey murkiness she expected, but it appeared viscous, like a silvery, grey oil of a vast quantity had been spilled turning the sea into a mercury expanse. Anna started to make her way to the breaking syrupy waves to investigate when she heard a noise, a child. At first it was muted but becoming more urgent, a child in distress? She attempted to locate the source, somewhere amongst the wind breakers, the sound was becoming louder, more panicked. "Please!" Was that right, please? A girl, very young and terrified. She began to make her way through the breakers, looking behind each one, it was hard to pinpoint exactly where the voice was coming from, the closer she seemed to get the further away the voice became. Terror began to rise in Anna's throat at the rate that the pitch of the voice increased, imparting a great distress. She had to find the child, she needed her. The sea of wind breaker colour began to blur in Anna's eyes, a pain forming at the side of her head. No! Anna stumbled into the breakers, feeling herself slipping away, into unconsciousness, she stumbled forward, a wooden strut jabbing into her ribs, causing a sharp intake of breath, more pain to add to the incessant throbbing in her head. She heard another voice, a male, angry, was he the source of the child's distress? "..ke ...itch". What was he saying, pain again in her ribs, she needed to get up, couldn't her arms were not responding, she was unable to move. "I SAID, WAKE UP BITCH!"

* * *

Bright lights, a man, Dave, oh god, reality. It flooded back, the situation that she was now in, the little girl was crying at the side of her, she had given up on the toys and sat with knees drawn up to her chest, huddling her legs, head down. Anna could not take her eyes off the girl, she wondered what had happened to her while she had been unconscious, she looked for signs that the girl was, at least physically, okay. Dave was watching her, he could see the concern for the girl in her eyes. A smile played across his lips and she sensed that intended to allow his cruelty to manifest in its fullest form. Desperate to buy some time she attempted to swallow her terror. "Dave, I need you to listen to me for a minute" Her voice was surprisingly calm and even, she felt as though she was watching a scene from some disturbing film, she the observer, detached from events that were playing out in front of her. Dave moved across the room to where the child was sitting "Go on Anna, get it off your chest" He had composed himself, now calm, considered. He crouched beside the child and began to stroke her hair, she didn't move away from him but looked up, beautiful eyes beseeching, asking why this was happening to her. In a frail voice the girl spoke "I want my mummy, I want to go home" The latter part of the sentence obliterated by a huge sob. Dave continued to stroke the girl's hair. "Shh, Anna has something to say sweetheart, let's hear what she has to say and then maybe we can take you home." The girl's gaze moved to Anna, pleading. "Dave, my colleagues know that I'm looking into you, the police know. I won't just "disappear" like the others. They'll make a connection and you'll be arrested. You'll go down for a very long time, do you understand what I'm saying?" Sweeping the child up into his large frame Dave sat her in his lap, he pulled the child towards his chest in an embrace that was painful, the girl winced and began choking on a sob. He was oblivious, glaring at Anna defiantly. "And that means what to me Anna? Do you think I give a fuck about your pathetic rules? I can tell you that I don't. I'm an animal, as are you, as is this girl, we are all here to serve a purpose and your purpose is my pleasure. It doesn't matter what you think about that, in your tiny little rule bound world, my reality is the only reality here. You and this lovely little creature here are actually quite privileged. Not only have you got my attention for the next few hours, maybe days if I can hold out that long, you are quite fine specimens after all" a wink and a smile, Anna began to realise that not only was this man a cruel and sadistic abuser but he was also completely insane. His tone and manner suggested that she should be grateful to him, this was completely unreal, Anna could feel herself disassociating from reality. Dave continued, "You will also be starring in a wonderful piece of art. My customers will marvel at your attempts to survive, at what the human body can take before it succumbs. I have many followers Anna, who appreciate the effort I put into my work, and they'll appreciate your contribution too. Think of it this way, you'll be providing a service much more appreciated than what you currently do, snatching babies and making sure feckless women keep their houses clean, come on Anna, what gives you the right to the moral high ground?" Dave continued to stroke the girl's hair, he sat her on the edge of the bed and looked directly into her eyes, touching her nose with his fingertip. "Oh dear, Anna isn't giving me a reason to take you back to your mummy is she?" His interaction with the girl would pass him off as a Sunday School teacher, no wonder he had managed to manipulate her mother.

Anna's state of disorientation was growing and she could not find the words to get out of the situation. Dave quickly drew his hand away from the girl's nose and pushed her hard against the bed, whimpering she clambered onto Anna's chest, burying her head in the crook of her arm. Anna drew the child's head closer with her chin, never taking her eyes off Dave. He had started to undress and was muttering something unheard under his breath. The girl began to cry, a despairing wail that seemed to come from her very soul, Dave paused and grinned at Anna "Music to my ears darlin." And then continued to undress. Now completely naked he walked around the side of the bed and leaned over, blocking out the bright light above Anna's head. He bent down and opened a drawer that was secreted in the bed base. Pulling something from the drawer he tussled, a mask onto his head, then a rattling, heavy objects clanking against each other, Anna shuddered when she realised the noise reminded her of her father rummaging around in his tool box, attempting to find an errant screwdriver to fix a plug.

Memories came racing back to her, vivid, like a west end play being presented in front of her eyes. Brief vignettes of love, warmth, security, shielded from the horrors of this world. Her parents called her a "chosen one" she had been adopted and always knew that this was the case, there was no secrecy, she was supported to look into her heritage, comforted when finding out she was the unwanted child of abusive alcoholics, feelings of gratitude that fate had brought her into the arms of these truly wonderful human beings. It couldn't end like this. She longed for the warmth of her infancy with every fibre of her being but there was no escape. Anna realised she had been hushing the little girl, a protective instinct taking over, wanting to convey some security to her, however pointless that might be in a situation like this. "Aw, look at you, quite the little mother aren't you. Well, before you get your go perhaps she ought to have hers first eh? We don't want you having all the fun do we?" Dave stood in front of the bed, resplendent, his face covered by a white rubber Halloween mask. Deep wrinkles and grotesque pale visage broken only by the black eyes that were visible through small slits. In his hand was a drill, he drew it up to his face and depressed the switch, the drill made an excruciatingly high patched noise that assaulted Anna's ears as if she had been physically beaten about her head. A surge of fear, the like she had never known rose up from the pit of her stomach and threatened to burst out of her mouth, sobbing and swallowing hard she forced it down. "This Anna, is my favourite toy, and I'm saving it for you." He placed the drill which to Anna had taken on an evil persona of it's own on a small console table to the left of the bed and then proceeded to pull out other devices from the bed drawer. Anna looked away, her mind had shifted from thoughts of escape, of rationalising with this inhuman thing before her to hoping her death and that of the girls would be swift, she had lost all hope. Dave finished setting up his "toys" and moved to the foot of the bed, he again checked the camera equipment and satisfied turned his attention to his captives, "let the games begin!" He grabbed the girl by the arm and yanked her from the bed. Anna, enraged pulled her legs up to her chest and kicked Dave in the stomach as hard as she possibly could. He let go of the girl and sprawled back against the adjacent wall, the wind knocked out of him. Scrabbling to his feet Anna literally saw his face change from pale to a livid red. He flew at her screaming "You fucking biiiiitttttch!" The final word drawn out like a battle cry. Anna flailed her legs in a vain attempt to keep him at bay, another sound entered the room, high pitched, deafening, it took her a second to realise it was her own scream. She closed her eyes, legs continued to kick into the air, not connecting with anything. This is it, oh god this is it, a mantra, spinning around in her head, or was she saying it out loud?

* * *

Her name "Anna?" it sounded like Charlie, had she lost consciousness again, no she couldn't, the girl, who would protect her, she had to wake up. She opened her eyes and knew she must be dreaming, Charlie was stood over her, the door to the hallway was open and there appeared to be several figures scuffling over something that was situated on the floor, out of her line of sight. "Anna, it's OK, you're OK." Charlie turned around and closed the door. He leaned over her and untied her hands, the reflection from his eyes was one of pity and grave concern. She felt sorry for him, whatever he was currently witnessing was a disturbing sight, something that would bring him nightmares in time to come. Yet, her heart was beginning to swell at the sight of him, the slow realisation that this was real, not a dream, Anna tried to speak but couldn't find any words, her throat hurt. She pulled the little girl towards her and hugged her as though both of their lives depended on it. She sat there, rocking back and forth on the bed for what seemed like an age, trying to make sense of what had happened, the hours that had just past seemed at once like decades and seconds. Finally Charlie spoke to her, "We need to get to the hospital Anna, you need to come with me" Anna was overcome, she loved Charlie then for allowing her some time to process, some time to hold the girl, trying to impress on her the tiniest hope that there was some decency in the world, something she would hopefully take from this terrifying experience and play it off against the dread that she would undoubtedly feel, every time she was alone, every time saw a man that slightly resembled Dave, every time she wanted to turn to a bottle or a needle to try and drown out the memories. Anna released her hold on the little girl who remained fixed to her chest, arms grasping Anna's sides. Charlie gently lifted her away, cooing and coaxing in gentle tones. Once hold of her, he held out a hand for Anna, the scuffling in the hallway had quietened. Anna stood, placed her hand in Charlie's palm, shakily at first and then gaining strength, resilience to face whatever may be on the other side of the door.

Chapter Twenty-eight

The hospital side ward was far too similar to the "chamber of nightmares" that Anna would sooner forget. She had threatened the irate nursing staff with discharging herself in an attempt to get the on call consultant to check her over so that she could leave this place. Charlie would be here in about forty five minutes. It was taking her much longer to dress than she had anticipated. Apparently she had had a dislocated shoulder, duly forced back into place, broken jawbone, two fractured ribs and multiple lacerations to her face. She wasn't looking forward to catching her reflection in a mirror any time soon. The pain killers were helping, despite her spaced out mind-set that was adding minutes to each thought she needed to process she knew without them the pain would be unbearable. All in good time, what she really needed was to know that David Cartwright had been arrested and charged. Charlie, where are you? How much longer would he be, checking her mobile phone it seem to take forever to figure out that he would be another thirty minutes. This was excruciating, she needed to get home, get to bed and sleep for a week, hopefully waking up capable of rational thought. Becoming vaguely aware that her feet were cold Anna glanced down. Her feet were bare, she was sure she had dressed herself, footwear included. She crawled onto the bed and began to cry, huge sobs that patients could probably hear two storeys above her. She didn't care, never had she felt so vulnerable, with so little control.

"Charlie please, hurry" a whisper through the sobs, she needed to get away from here.

Chapter Twenty-nine

"We're really glad to have you on board Anna, let me show you to your desk" Immediately impressed, an office that had dedicated work spaces rather than a "hot desking" policy was a huge thumbs up as far as Anna was concerned. ""I'll take you around to meet the team and then we can have some time to look at your induction and cases that I've set aside for you. Yeah?" "Yes, that's fine." She responded with a gentle laugh. The new manager of the agency post she had taken up was clearly an old style social worker, wanting to get the staff on board, wanting to make them feel valued and part of the team. Anna realised that even as an agency worker she would benefit from the nurturing approach her new manager, Cindy espoused.

It had been three long months since her encounter with Dave in the flat. She almost immediately decided that she needed to move on, that her office, her colleagues, her manager, even her desk would constantly remind her of the trauma, and she didn't want to become a slave to it. So, on a whim, and while still on sick leave from work, she had handed in her resignation. She had then signed up to various agencies and decided to accept this, her current post. A twelve month contract with a mental health team, how difficult could it be? She needed a break from the incessant barrage of the abuse of children that was threatening to strip her of her compassion and trust in the goodness of humanity. Supporting individuals with their depression, their anxiety. The common woes that affect us all would be a welcome relief to the darkness that she had endured for so many years. She had woken up this morning with a new found enthusiasm for her work, she was energized and sure she would be able to make a difference. Anna smiled and Cindy noticed this "Anna, you're like a breath of fresh air, I think you'll find that many of the workers are feeling the pressure, you know, the government cuts, more clients, no extra staff, but it's all about attitude yeah? I'm sure your years in child protection have developed some... erm, resilience?" "Indeed, I would imagine it has, so cases, do you have a list?" Cindy clapped her hands together, "Yes, let's go into my office, you can meet the staff later."

Anna had never worked for an agency before but the offices she had worked in had employed them. They were truly the workhorses of any Local Authority. In some teams the agency staff were accepted as part of the team, enjoying all of the training, meetings and additional morsels of project work that kept the mind active and motivation flowing. She had also worked in teams where the agency workers were presented with a massive caseload on day one and expected to get their heads down and plough through it, no concessions, no carrots dangling on any sticks, even a lunch break would be frowned upon by target driven managers. She contemplated which camp she would fall into with this current post. Cindy seemed pretty nice, an old school hippy dippy worker, but appearances could be deceptive, time would tell. At this current moment Anna was happy to be out with the old and in with the new. She followed Cindy into her office, it was shared with several other managers, her desk appeared overloaded and a heap of files ready to cascade over the side and onto the already messy floor. Piles of journals lay in less than neat stacks, Community Care, British Journal of Social Work, and stacks of print outs of policies and procedures, articles of interest. "Do you actually get the time to read these?" Anna picked up the nearest article "Mental Capacity Act versus Mental Health Act: Pathways to appropriate use of Deprivation of Liberty Safeguards". Cindy surveyed her paper empire and dramatically threw her arms in the air "I try Anna, I really do, but one can only fit onto a spoon what one can fit onto a spoon," She smiled as if this completely satisfied the question. "Ok, cases, you wanted cases, here they are. I've taken the liberty of prioritising, but of course, you're an experienced worker, do what you think you need to do. There are twenty five on the list to start with. These are all priority cases we haven't been able to allocate but we have a huge backlog and I expect that once you have settled in and made inroads with these, you'll be able to take more." Anna surveyed the list she had been presented with, at least she knew which camp she was in, workhorse. The names were a blur, a brief synopsis of the case couldn't fully convey the complexities of the lives that were hidden behind the list. "There is one particular case I'm concerned about, a young woman with post-partum depression. She's had a history of mental health issues, intermittent engagement with services. Child protection are involved, hence the reason I thought you would be ideal to pick up the case, with your experience of course. Paige Connor, if you wouldn't mind having a look at that one first? Meantime, I've filled in your diary with a brief induction, and Anna, welcome!" Cindy beamed, Anna's heart sank.

Chapter Thirty

DI Cooper sat across the table from Dave Cartwright in the interview room come stationery supply depository. The beige paint was flaking from several parts of the wall, a reminder that government cuts were not just relegated to the police force. He regarded the man in front of him with a non-judgemental yet intense gaze that Dave clearly found uncomfortable. The silence had lasted for over two minutes. Dave pushed his chair back with a slow, excruciating screech and rose to his feet "If your not gonna speak to me Cooper, I may as well go back to my cell." Dave nodded at the guard that screened the door to the interview room. The guard ignored Dave and looked to the DI for guidance. "Okay, Okay" Dave gave DI Cooper the hard stare, "What do you want?" "C'mon Dave, sit down, you know what I want. First things first though, how is going? How are they treating you here?" Dave regarded DI Cooper for a long moment, he gave a quiet, supercilious laugh, "Are you serious? You've come here, to see me and ask me about my wellbeing? I know enough about the misanthropic nature of humans to realise that this is not what you want to fucking know DI Cooper, a bit of honesty, please?" "Fair enough Dave, if you want to get right down to it I want to know if there were any more victims? I want you to tell me what you've been doing for the last few years. I've come here for a chat, giving you the opportunity to get it all off your chest. If that isn't something you want to do then I have officers that will come and question you, which I'm sure you know is a completely different kettle of fish. What I want to know is your side of the story, what you really have to say. We know there are others Dave, and if I'm honest, I want you to start right at the beginning, with your family, your mum, your dad and your sister. Why don't you start there?" "Hmm, really? And what do I get out of this, let's say, hypothetically, I'm able to have a little chat with you, assist you in closing a few open cases, what's in it for me?" "A clear conscience Dave, the knowledge that even though you have committed these awful crimes, you could at least help the victims' families know what's happened. That's what you'd get out of it." Dave rocked back on the flimsy plastic chair, back and forth, back and forth for several minutes, contemplating the request. DI Cooper leaned forward on the table between them. "I'm going to level with you Dave, we are currently conducting an investigation and gathering information around several open cases that you are linked with. It's a matter of time until we bring charges." DI Cooper felt he was taking a few liberties with his last statement, they had a few old leads that they were following up but the chances were they wouldn't be able to muster enough of a case to get the CPS to accept it. Sadly, they needed something more from Dave in order to progress with the other cases. "The thing is Cooper, I might be able to give you something but I'm not sure I can open up to you," a mock sadness spread across his face, "I like women as you know, I wonder if the lovely Anna would come and talk to me. She makes me feel, erm, secure, do you know what I mean? I think I just might be able to open up to her." Dave grinned, he clearly knew he was grating on DI Cooper's moral compass.

***

"You don't have to do this Anna. I appreciate the ordeal you've been through. I want you to take some time. Talk to your manager, your partner." The DI was genuine, she knew that, but the words were out of her mouth with a conviction that surprised her before she realised they were being formed in her mind. "I'll do it. These people, victims, need to be found. If I'm the only one he'll talk to, for whatever perverse reason that might be, then I'll do it." She looked DI Cooper straight on with an unswerving resolve. "What else can he do to me?" She shrugged her shoulders. Cooper regarded Anna with a curious look, he had nothing but admiration for her. He had obviously had his scrapes with the criminals he pursued, but his interactions were after the fact. He, unlike her, had never had to face a criminal that had set out to rape and murder him and video the process for posterity. No, she was a strong woman and he was grateful. His main objective was to bring closure to the souls that had lost and were in a purgatory, unable to make sense of a loved one's passing. If Anna was strong enough to assist he was more than grateful, but he wouldn't pressure her, she had suffered her own hell. "I want you to think about it Anna. Give me a call tomorrow when you've had time to mull it over." She attempted to reiterate her impulsive decision but he thwarted her. "I'm serious. Talk to someone, and don't get back to me until you do."

* * *

Later that night Anna sat in her comfy chair, an extremely large glass of pinot noir in her hand, the second. Her head was in a mess, two halves arguing, yes, do it, no don't. She could come up with reasons for both but found her mind was going around in circles. She picked up mobile phone from the coffee table. Desperately longing to call her father. He wouldn't answer her, his advice and guidance was now relegated to memory. What would he suggest? She debated this for the umpteenth time in the last sixty minutes. He would have said yes, do it, and he would have said no. Her fingers lazily found Charlie's number. A depressed green phone symbol later she was listening to a connecting call. "Anna, is everything Ok?" Charlie sounded concerned, it was twelve thirty, she should have realised. "I'm sorry Charlie, I need to talk to you. I thought I'd be able to do this on my own, but I can't." Her words faltered, she realised she was close to a full on sob, breathing in her emotion, "It's Ok, I... I'm Ok. God, I'm sorry, I didn't realise the time…" Help me out Charlie, please. He read her thoughts. "I'm coming over, be with you in about twenty minutes." He hung up. She wondered why things couldn't stay the same, she had a life, a career that she loved, for all its faults. Then this. This man, monster, had ripped open a wound that she had no hope would heal. It had thrust her into the stark reality of inhumanity. Perhaps she had been affected by this at one point in time and it had become the norm. The cases she had to deal with were sickening by any other's standards. Perhaps she had become immune, and now this, she had been a "victim" had received the torment that she believed she had expressed empathy with towards her clients. Knowing now that this was not the case she lamented all of the lives she had touched, had attempted to support, to heal. She had been totally inadequate in her approach. The complete and utter violation she had experienced had ultimately struck a blow that had created a new, fresh reality. She was usually the third person in her cases, the one that picked up the mess, the aftermath. Not the one to experience things first hand. Another gulp of wine, liquid diazepam. Dad, I need you.

She was about to pour another glass when the doorbell chimed, it was nineteen minutes since her call to Charlie ended. She opened the door and he immediately entered, pulling Anna into a bear hug. "You Ok?" She smiled at him, an expression that told him she was far from Ok. "Wine?" "Of course, we can't have you drinking on your own like a saddo, can we? Just think of the headlines." Gentle voice, gentle smile, Charlie, you make me feel so much better. She poured two, very large glasses, draining the bottle. They settled on the sofa. "Tina's been at it again." Charlie referred to the rude and hilarious office worker. "Who has she upset now?" Anna smiled, genuinely amused, the minutiae of the office politics was a welcome relief from the decisions to be made. "Just about everyone, apparently she now no longer types, can you believe that, a secretary that doesn't type. The team are up in arms about it. Unison are involved. Crazy. Where do people get the time to deliberate these trivial things?" Charlie shook his head, an incredulous grin on his face, one eyebrow raised. Anna laughed, a genuine laugh. "Also, you might like this, half an hour of the team meeting was taken up by Pat and Cath complaining about the lack of liquid soap in the toilets, apparently a bar of soap is unhygienic?" "Can you believe that I miss it Charlie? The new team are great but I'm just not involved in the periphery, I'm agency, so it's work, work, work." "Are you in work at the moment, I presumed you'd taken a bit of time off considering?" "Yes I have, a few days." Anna recounted the conversation she had with her new manager, explaining the dilemma she was in regarding Dave, needing a few days off to think about it. Her erstwhile positive and encouraging manager was not quite as supportive as she anticipated. An "almost" argument ensued and Anna had demanded some time off. Cindy responding with something along the lines of Anna should have been experienced enough to take it in her stride. Reflecting on this, Anna surmised that Cindy had never, in her experience, been knocked out, bound, stripped naked, almost raped and beaten by a psychopath, and thus had been unable to draw on any empathy of Anna's situation. Not being desperate for cash, cancelled leave and holiday for several years had left her with a little extra to draw upon in difficult times. Anna had left the office, telling her manager that she would take some time, if they wanted to replace her, go for it, but she would take it up with the General Social Care Council. She had left Cindy stood in her office with an open mouth and a resolve to contact HR. "So Charlie, what do you think I should do?" Charlie looked at her for a few moments, his look was intense, searching her face for the answer to her own question. He found none. "What are your thoughts so far?" Not answering, Anna hooked her arm around Charlie's neck and pulled him towards her, she needed a distraction, something that was instinctive rather than based in rational, logical thought. She didn't think about the consequences of her actions, she and Charlie had liaisons previously, they were compatible, he could offer her some kind of psychological sanctuary she now needed. He responded to her wishes eagerly and talk of her dilemma quickly gave way to a physical catharsis.

Chapter Thirty-one

Dave lay on his cell bed, not luxurious but not uncomfortable. His surroundings didn't particularly bother him, Dave was the kind of person who lived behind the eyes, his inner world was more real to him. The outside world, reality, provided him the material to entertain himself. That was what he doing now, reliving the experiences he had had with the lovely Anna, all the more sweet for not fulfilling his desires. But she wouldn't escape the end he had planned for her. He would deconstruct her, break her down in a manner more ferocious than had she allowed him his pleasure at the flat. When his plan was fulfilled, the lovely Anna would have wished that he had killed her, spared her the horror she was about to fall into. He had no doubts she would succumb to his plan, he had read her, she wouldn't be able to resist the possibility of helping the poor grieving families. Her ego! It equalled his, the opposite side of the coin granted, but equal in capacity for grandiosity. He knew she would fall into his trap, of course he knew, they were basically the same, it was simply a matter of time. The conversation he had with Cooper would pave the way. Dave had deliberated, accurately, that Cooper would mull over his offer, initially dismissing it out of hand. But the seed was planted, solve a few open cases, lay a few ghosts to rest, then Cooper would put the ball in the Social Worker's court, it would be up to her, no pressure. She would wrestle with it for another couple of days, and then voila, she would be delivered to him like a lamb to the proverbial slaughter. Beautiful, educated Anna, she needed to be put in her place, needed some instruction, he had missed the opportunity once, it wouldn't happen again. He would wait, and wait, but they would come back to him. While he waited, he would play over and over in his mind his experiences so far, that would be enough, for now. Dave closed his eyes, retreating to his reality, the world beyond his mind was a construct, a cage, with impossible rules and fake people. His head contained the truth, the gut wrenching reality that was this life, his head and not forgetting his films of course, doors that opened onto the maelstrom. Images and sounds filled his head, he decided not to choose one, single, scenario but allow everything to flood his head, assault his senses, high pitched screams, low gurgles, sticky red blobs flying through the air, spattering his bared skin like warm, heavy rain, a final exhale, forcing out the remaining life force. A smile crept upon his face.

* * *

DI Cooper clicked off his mobile. He felt pretty awful about asking the Social Worker to meet with Dave, resolving that he had not in fact asked her, rather he provided her with information and left her with the decision as to what to do with it. Regardless, it was a bloody awful dilemma to resolve. Had he worked with her previously, developed some kind of relationship he believed that he would be able to counsel her through the decision making process, as it was, he had hoped she would be able to gain the support and guidance of those she chose to. He reflected on what little he did know of her. She was a woman that would put her own safety on the line to protect children, she researched David Cartwright, put all of the pieces together before presenting to an inept CPU. As far as he was aware they were still bumbling along, hadn't yet followed up her leads, she had taken it upon herself, foolhardy as this turned out to be, to investigate David Cartwright. She was clearly made of determined stuff. He believed, no, hoped, she would do the right thing. But if she didn't, he wouldn't blame her, the poor woman had been through enough. He had done his duty, the ball was now firmly in her court. He would accept any decision, without judgment, gladly having crossed paths with an individual that had shown a fortitude he wished some of his own officers possessed. The DI's wife popped her head around the study door "Dinner's ready." A pause and raised left eyebrow, "Are you alright?" "I'm fine my love, it's been a difficult day that's all. I'll be right with you."

DI Cooper's wife returned to the kitchen, she sat at the large oak dining table, waiting for her husband. The children were otherwise engaged this evening, it was just the two of them. She had been hoping for some pleasant conversation and the usual agenda item, which her husband would confide in her the burden that he carried with him through his working hours. Knowing this would never happen she fixed a cheery smile on her face in anticipation of his presence at the dinner table. She hoped at the very least to counterbalance the work that he did, inject some normality and pleasantries into his life. He had dedicated himself to the force, and to herself and the children. She had as much admiration as she had love for him. Often she had conversations with her friends, talk of errant husbands, approaching their middle age, chasing girls that were young enough to be their grandchildren, let alone daughters. Whether these were physical affairs or just wishful thinking, the DI's wife could not imagine such a situation. She had sympathy for her friends but the tales also instilled in her pride. Her husband had an integrity and loyalty that would appear to be rare amongst her circle, if ever there was a truly decent man it was he, her husband. The cheery smile she fixed on her face was now replaced with one of genuine warmth. He popped his head around the door, "Sorry" his eyes fixed on her and he knew that everything would be fine.

Chapter Thirty-two

"Given the dearth of edible substances in your kitchen I decided to go to the café and get some bacon butties. Here." Rubbing eyes with her knuckles Anna peeped over her quilt to find Charlie proffering a sandwich and a mug of tea. As a rule she didn't eat breakfast, copious amounts of tea and coffee yes, but food? Not wanting to appear rude she sat up and took the meal. "Thanks" A grin that was reciprocated. "Charlie, I…" "Don't say anything, just eat your butty before it gets cold. I'm going to have to call at the office for an hour but then I'll come back. Before you start this isn't negotiable. So eat, shower, get yourself sorted out and I'll be back before you know it." An almost inaudible laugh escaped her lips, she nodded "Yes sir." and sipped her tea. He could almost read her mind, she was on the verge of apologising, yet again, for her weakness last night, asserting there was nothing in it. But he made her feel better, safer and happier than she had in a while. She also had deliberations to make that would benefit from his input, she valued his opinion and was comforted by his support. Charlie had left and she was alone in her silent house, the odd twitter of a bird that she assumed must be perched on a willow tree in her back garden, oblivious to the shit that occupied its world. She was suddenly overwhelmed by his leaving and realised she needed him, no, she didn't need him, wanted him with her. The complexities of their relationship could be contemplated at a later date, right now she was glad he was returning and that was enough.

Anna focused on her instructions, glad for some direction in a time that had caused her to flounder from day to day. She had believed the new job would take her mind off things, and it had until the call from Cooper. She realised the job was a fragile protection and it would possibly have delayed her eventual break down. Maybe this was the best way, to confront her demons now. Deal with it and then move on, whole. Not this fragmented woman lying in her bed after nine, deliberating a prescription for anti-depressants, changing jobs, vulnerable, her previous strength needed to be re-established. She ate her sandwich, finished her tea and then showered, wanting to impress Charlie when he returned with her old smile and candid, rational conversation. Did it matter that the source of her strength was another person, him? She decided not. She rationalised that humans are social animals, they depend on others for all kinds of things, given her current dilemma, she was entitled to this moment of weakness.

He returned as he said he would. Filling her in on the convoluted attempts to get some leave and reorganise his diary, much to the chagrin of Tina, who, incidentally, refused to reorganise his visits for him. Charlie related his tale with a flourish, intending to relieve some of the tension hanging over Anna. "Jean sends her regards, I actually think I saw some real emotion on her face when she asked after you?" "Lack of sleep Charlie, you're clearly hallucinating." They both laughed. "You look better

Anna, another cuppa?" She nodded her head and thought about how she would be able to make the decision she needed to make. On the one hand it should have been very simple. If it were in her power to help the families of other victims seek some justice, lay their lost souls to rest, then she should do it, without hesitation. In order to do this, to perform this very basic justice she would need to sit in the same room with, talk to, the monster that had invaded her sleep every single night since the incident. The thought of it was terrifying. This was an animal who was going to kill her and the innocent young girl, kill them, end their lives. The words were bandied around in so many magazines, films, documentaries that it was difficult to reconcile the simple collection of letters to the abject terror this thought conjured in her. The sick feeling in the pit of her stomach, the hairs raised on the back of her neck, the feeling of some unknown doom about to descend over her. She didn't hear Charlie come back into the living and almost knocked the mug out of his hand when he spoke to her. "Be careful Anna" he admonished her gently. "I can't live like this Charlie, I'm frightened every second of every day. I'm trying, I really am, sometimes I feel that I've managed to get my shit together and then boom! I start to think about it, I have a nightmare, something reminds me, I'm just about hanging on." Anna had shocked herself, she wouldn't allow the words to come out previously, she didn't want her feelings out there, spoken and given weight, making them real. But they were out now, dancing around in front of her, taunting her. Tears, sobs, the last few months of pent up emotion erupting at that point, she didn't believe she would ever stop. Charlie held her in his arms, knowing that this outburst of emotion was a long time coming. They sat together for a long time, until eventually the sobs became less frequent and then subsided altogether.

Chapter Thirty-three

The DI smiled, a concerned yet incredibly grateful smile at Anna. They were in the waiting room of the prison that Dave was languishing on remand. She felt oppressed, the high walls and overwhelming security spoke of a need to contain, to control. Of course, this was a prison, what did she expect? She rationalised that she didn't expect to feel like a prisoner along with the other inmates. A guard broke the hushed tones of the waiting room. He burst through the door with a deafening jangling of keys. "Detective Inspector Cooper and Anna Black?" They both quickly stood to attention. "A quick word, Mr Cartwright is stating he will only see Ms Black, is that alright with you inspector?" Anna raised an eyebrow, a questioning, maybe it isn't alright with me, expression on her face. The stony guard didn't even glance her way. Cooper, looking a little embarrassed at his brethren in gender's clear disregard of Anna and her opinions gave her a grave look. "It's entirely up to you Anna, you won't be on your own in there, you can leave any time you like and I'll be waiting here for you." "Well, I'm here now, let's see what he has to say for himself, eh?" She hoped her nonchalant words didn't betray the anxiety that was taking hold of her, she was trembling, felt nauseous and couldn't think of a single place on earth that she would rather be than here right now. "Thank you." It was a simple but heart felt statement, he was depending on her and she couldn't let him down.

The guard led her through to the visiting room. A large room with several tables, some empty, some occupied by prisoners and their visitors, deep in conversation, fixed on one another. There were several guards positioned around the perimeter of the room. Anna hesitated when see spotted Dave, his arms were resting on the table in front of him, fingers loosely intertwined, head slightly bowed. She absurdly had the idea of a man contemplating his next move in a game of chess, perhaps not so absurd given the circumstances. Anna glanced up at the guard who nodded for her to approach Dave.

Be strong Anna, be strong, her father's voice inside her head. A deep breath, she boldly marched up to the table and pulled back the chair with an audible scrape, no one appeared to notice but the sound made her cringe, reverberating in her head. She sat with a heavy determination. Dave didn't immediately look up but instead appeared to inspect his fingernails, a curiosity he had only just discovered. The sight of this, this evil personified, demanding her presence, expecting to maintain her terror and then arrogantly not even acknowledging the fact that she had turned up to meet the man. It suddenly occurred to her that he was imprisoned, and she was, as a result safe, a bolt from the blue. The evil before her now appeared pathetic, arrogance had overtaken him and this was the situation he found himself in. Separated from society, from friends, from family, assuming he had any. She was in the position of control. Not him. How stupid of her, all of the sleepless nights, the haunting shadows, jumping at her own reflection. This was the real Dave, a prisoner, behind bars, contained as she had felt earlier, but she could leave this place. He didn't have that luxury, the only control he had over her was self-imposed. At this realisation she let out a sigh and shook her head, this imitation of a person was not going to have any kind of hold over her for one second longer. She decided to play him at his own game, turning her attention to the other individuals in the room, she feigned disinterest in him, she caught a guards eye and smiled. She glanced at her watch, it worked. He finally tilted his head level with hers "Hello Anna" a thick inflection, a half flirtatious, half annoyed grin on his face.

* * *

"I'm not all bad you know Anna." The sickening leer was augmented on what would generally be regarded as a handsome face. "You could consider my childhood, it wasn't the best" She remained silent. "I want to help, I really do. I just keep getting this thought in my head, I feel like I need to help you see the light, lead you to an...epiphany, yes, an epiphany, do you know what I mean? Your work takes you to the fringes, but not into the heart of it, into the reality of what life really is." Anna was resolute in her silence, she regarded Dave with dead eyes, conveying nothing. A slight, almost imperceptible shift in his demeanour. "How's the boyfriend doing, he's a lucky guy Anna, I wish I was in his shoes." A sickening grin spreading across his face, he leaned a little closer to her, not enough to draw the attention of the wardens, but enough, she stood her ground, not moving an inch, cold stare fixed upon a grim face. A whisper "I took the liberty of calling around to your house, just wanted to check on you, make sure everything was ok, you know? Your fella turned up, quite a show you put on there, kept me up all night it did." He leaned back in his seat, self satisfied, waiting for her shock, her disgust as his violation. "And, what Dave?" She retorted in a surprisingly calm, cool voice. "So you're a peeping tom as well as everything else, sorry to disappoint but this doesn't really surprise me." Anna was overawed by her calm, she wanted to scream and literally fly across the table to erase this freak out of her life for ever. Think of the victims, this is why I'm here. "Hmm, ok, you're a tough one, I'll give you that. You might be more interested if I were to tell you that I recorded the whole thing, for my own personal use of course. I kind of got to thinking though, this is too good, I'm not a selfish man, maybe I ought to share it." Anna's stare remained cold. "This is where you have to decide, cos I'm gonna offer you a deal, are you interested?" He sat back, rocking in the chair, weird grin back on his face. "Dave" it was Anna's turn to lean across the table, invading his personal space as he had done with her. "I came here at the request of DI Cooper, a man who I have known for a short space of time but admire considerably. He stated to me that you wanted to, er, confess. Have I been given the wrong impression? If so, I may as well leave now."

In hushed tones "I have a lock up, I store my artwork there if you see what I mean." Cogs whirred, evidence. Is he telling the truth? He was arrogant enough to believe she would go along with it. "So, you want me to get your...artwork? Seriously, what do you want?" "I'm giving you the opportunity to retrieve your very own high definition film to do with what you will. Believe me when I say I'm a man of my word, there is only one copy and it's yours. Get rid of it, watch it with your boyfriend, the choice is yours." Anna glanced around at the guards, no one appeared to be paying them any particular attention. "But it comes at a very small price. I want you to watch the other films and then come back to see me. If you do, then I'll tell you whatever it is you want to know, names, dates, whatever." He watched her intently. Could see the effort she was putting into finding a way around his offer. "The lock up won't be found Anna, I hired it under a different name. And the films, the films are anonymous shall we say, if the police were to get hold of them it wouldn't give them anything to go on. Come on, why wouldn't you do this, it's a public service." He laughed and rocked back on his chair.

"Okay, I'll do it, where's the lock up?" Dave grinned, the most sickening grin through the exchange, As he told Anna the whereabouts of the lock up he returned his attention to his fingernails, a little prodding and poking in a manner that Anna would not have noticed save her heightened sense of awareness created by being in this man's presence, he lifted a tiny piece of paper from his right, middle fingernail. Deftly secreting it under his palm he slid his hand halfway across the table. "You'll need this for both locks."

She starred into his eyes, his soul, nothing, he was dead on the inside, it was like looking into the eyes of a deer that had been the unfortunate victim of a less than careful driver. His victims needed a voice, and fate had dictated that she would be the one to deliver that voice, if this whole thing was a charade then so be it, at least she would have tried. If she took the impossibly small piece of paper there was the chance that some resolution could be found. If she dismissed it and passed on the content of her conversations with Dave to the DI then there was a chance that resolution would never be found. Her mind was made up in a matter of seconds. She placed a hand, incredibly steady on the table and moved it towards his, she didn't speak, the action was more than enough to give him an answer. The exchange was made. No guard approached, no one appeared to notice that a transaction with the devil had just taken place.

"I'm sorry, he just didn't tell me anything, more concerned with messing with my head." "Anna, I'm sorry, I truly am, I shouldn't have asked you to do this, it was a long shot." Anna smiled at Cooper, "It's Ok, seriously, it was worth a try, eh? Anyone would have done the same." Anna paused, feeling an incredible wave of guilt at her deception, dashing Cooper's hopes. "It's all a game to him, I would imagine that when he gets a little bored he'll ask me, or you for that matter to come back, give us snippets of information, it's all about the control. Don't worry, it's a matter of time." A conciliatory smile. "Anna, you've done enough, more than most would in your position, and I thank you for it. Let's get you home." The DI's words made her want to cry, for his humanity and graciousness, she gave in, the tears forcing their way out of her eyes with no regard to the strong and stoic facade she was attempting to uphold. Cooper looked at her with sympathy, compassion, this only made her worse, she was deceiving him, holding back on information that he needed, making her feel like a fake, a liar. "Could you get me a taxi please", each word punctuated by a half sob. Anna couldn't trust herself to make it all of the way home without divulging to Cooper what she knew. "Are you sure Anna, I can take you home?" Concern in his inflections, "I just need some time on my own, some time to think." DI Cooper seemed to mull things over for a moment, did he know she was lying? Regardless, he relented, "Of course you do. You know you can call me anytime Anna. You have my personal mobile, anytime, seriously." She looked at DI Cooper, closely, and for longer than would normally be acceptable, a subconscious plea, ask me, take away this burden. The look ended in a "Yes, of course, thank you. I'm going to wait outside, I need some air." The DI watched her go, he had a niggling feeling that she wasn't telling him the whole story. But he had a good feeling about Anna, if she was keeping something from him it was for a good reason, the truth would out.

* * *

Anna retrieved the tiny scrap of paper from her jeans pocket. She was amazed that this exchange had actually occurred without detection and it made her acutely aware of how prison life operated. The paper turned out to be a cigarette paper, extremely thin and easily folded into a miniscule scrap. She carefully unfolded it, 6629, the numbers had been written in a biro, were inmates allowed biros? Clearly they were. So this was the combination to his sins. Was she prepared to unlock this Pandora's Box of sickness? Come on Anna, too late to turn back now. She had deceived the DI, felt awful about it. Now she had to get the evidence that Cooper desperately needed to make sure Cartwright stayed behind bars for a very long time. She would be foolish to jeopardise his game. If she played it they would all have what they needed and his arrogance would backfire. The taxi pulled up and she got in, the long drive back to her home gave her plenty of time to think about the exchange with Dave, and fill her with a resolve to end this whole terrible episode in her life, and that of the individuals that had had the misfortune of being on his destructive, sadistic path.

To her surprise Charlie was still in her house when she returned. She was simultaneously glad and annoyed by this. Charlie, yet again, appeared to read her mind. "I thought you might need some company so I kinda hung around, hope you don't mind. If you need to be on your own I'll get going." He looked at her a little sheepishly, clearly realising he had crossed some boundaries by staying at her house without any clear agreement. "Do you know what Charlie? I should be really bloody annoyed but strangely I'm not." She laughed, as much to herself than for Charlie's benefit. "It's good that your here, seriously, I need to talk to someone, to you. But you need to keep this to yourself, ok?"

Charlie guided Anna to the sofa and she proceeded to divulge the events of the day, the conversation with Dave, the emotional roller coaster of facing up to him, the potential for some resolution. He listened, did not interrupt, allowed her to get it out of her system. Eventually she sat back on the sofa, and looked at him, waiting for some kind of response. "Have you told Cooper about all of this?" Simply a question, no judgment in the inflection, but the space between them injected an admonishment into the words. Before responding Anna took stock, she felt bad for not informing Cooper and she couldn't project this onto Charlie's innocent question. "No, I didn't want anything to get in the way of getting some evidence on this guy." Charlie looked thoughtful for a moment, rubbing his chin, "I'll come with you to the lock up."

"I want to go alone, I don't know Charlie, I feel like I need to deal with this on my own, put it to bed, do you know what I mean?" Anna examined her nails abstractly, this brought back an HD version of Dave in the visitor's hall, she quickly tucked her hands underneath her legs. "Yes, I do understand, but at the same time, what if there's some kind of trap, something weird, I don't know Anna, I just don't think you should go alone."

She had already considered these issues, maybe Dave had associates who would be lying in wait, a booby trap perhaps. But she really didn't believe this was the case. She intrinsically felt that Dave wanted to inflict some damage on her, he wanted to play his games. She had gotten away, and for Dave this was not acceptable. He needed to punish her in some way, but it was he that needed this. Not an associate, he needed to feel that he had control over her, directly, not via some other weirdo that would reap the benefits of her torment.

"I can see what you're saying, but I'm going to do this on my own. It's weird I know, and Charlie, thank you for supporting me. I'll give you a call later, when I get back, ok?" Charlie sighed, he knew he was doing the wrong thing, it completely went against the grain but gave in none the less.

"Look, if you haven't contacted me by eleven I'm calling Cooper. One thing I'm going to need to know, and I'm serious Anna, where's the lock up?" Charlie's grave expression filled her with something, not love, fondness, an overwhelming desire to comfort, to reassure, but she couldn't do that. All she managed was a description that she had been given by Dave. The location of the lock up, it was familiar to her and would be to Charlie. "When all of this is over Charlie, I think we need to go on a date." She uttered a thin laugh, a hope that at some point, this would actually would be over.

Chapter Thirty-four

It seemed befitting that Anna was entering the lock up in the dead of night, alone. This was going to be an awful experience, she knew it, the darkness and solitude would amplify it, but it also felt that she was coming to the end of a horrifying journey that she had started on her own and so should finish it in the same way. She had to beat Dave, whatever psychological torture he had in store for her, and she knew that's exactly what it would be, embracing and overcoming it would defeat him. He wouldn't get what he wanted and would languish in his four walls tormented that his last chance at cruelty was denied. She examined the combination lock and the numbers that she had recited in her head since their discussion came back to her. Depressing each numbered button with an audible click she half expected that the lock wouldn't open. That this was an elaborate hoax, designed to torment the victims' families into greater depths of suffering. It clicked open. A quick look around, still alone, she entered the lock up. It was very dark, thin tendrils of washed out light crept over objects as yet unknown like spiders legs. A rough wall on her left yielded a familiar square protrusion and she flicked on the light switch. A fluorescent flickered eventually settled to bath lock up with harsh white light.

She glanced around the room noting the incredibly ordinary items that appeared surreal given the nature of her visit. A beautiful print, a sweater, mundane items that would be found in any home. How could such a man, no, monster have such ordinary, innocent possessions? What had she expected to find, pentacles and a doorway to hell? Despite her fear Anna was becoming annoyed with herself, focus! You know why you're here, get on with it and get out of this place. Her matriarchal inner voice admonished her and it moved her forward into the room. She quickly found the safe, an old style reinforced box of secrets. As promised the combination was correct, she pulled open the heavy door with closed eyes, opening them very slowly in order to blur any horror that might lurk in the shadows. Boxes eventually came into focus, lots of them, some familiar DVD cases others appeared to be the old style video cassettes. He had stated that the image he had sickeningly taken of her and Charlie was a DVD so she could ignore the videos. Having not had the forethought to bring something with her to carry the boxes in she found a plastic shopping bag amongst the bric-a-brac and emptied the safe of its DVD collection. With a sudden urgency she forced down a wave of panic and quickly made her way out of the lock up. In the safety of her car she slapped down the driver's side lock which secured the whole car. She let out a long, audible breath, realising she had been holding it for some time, like a scuba diver swimming in deep, dangerous waters. Feeling the comforting whir of the engine she made her way through the dark, deserted streets back to her home.

* * *

A neat pile of DVD's that were scrawled with the names of popular films laid to her right, the remote control to her left, she sat in front of her television. It was set to the DVD channel but the screen indicated there was no DVD in the player to be viewed. Anna sat like this for what could have been minutes, could have been hours. Anna had text Charlie when she had returned home. Her part of the bargain, she had contemplated inviting him over but decided he was best left out of this. She hadn't told him about the possibility of an "Anna and Charlie" sex tape and for some reason found the idea of encountering it in the midst of what were most likely going to be child pornography films contaminating, abhorrent beyond the imaginable. Frozen in a tableau of dread. "The Green Mile" it slid into the player and a familiar tune started to play, "Welcome to the jungle, we've got fun and games..." the tune continued but Anna couldn't tear her eyes from the floor. Nearing the end the song faded out and she could hear a faint sob, some kind of electrical tool, a drill? An ear piercing scream, Anna covered her ears, trying to drown out the sounds she knew would haunt her. The remote, she fumbled for it but it wouldn't stay in her hands, it was as though she had smeared them with butter, more music Lou Reed's Venus in Furs, the disjointed, hypnotic rhythm of the tune added to the surreal state she was in. She had to look at the screen, tearing her eyes from the floor she forced herself to view the image. A woman, about Anna's age, tied to a familiar bed in a familiar room, a look of fright and confusion on her contorted face, Anna was sure she could make out freckles on the woman's face but realised with a nauseous churn in her stomach that the tiny spots were flecks of blood. The woman wore a tattered fur coat, pale, naked flesh exposed beneath it, rivulets of crimson blood were trickling from a number of wounds dotted around her body. A puddle had formed in her navel, spilling periodically when she writhed. A naked man appeared on the scene, his back to the camera, he lunged at the woman, waving a drill in front of her eyes, her screams were mercifully drowned by the eerie music. Anna could not see his face but she knew who he was, a band separated his hair at the back of his head, he wore a mask. A lunge forced the drill into the woman's right thigh, her expression more contorted than before, he turned to the camera and held up the drill, blood and flesh flying from it and covering his bare chest. Arms clenched in a warped body builder's stance, posing for the camera, the ugly Halloween mask glaring fixedly. Anna noticed a doll in the corner of the screen, it was dressed in what appeared to be some kind of frilly party frock, arms and legs bent at awkward angles beneath a plume of pink frills and bouncy, curled hair. More blood, a patch of it blooming from the hidden face, not a doll, a girl. Slumped on the floor like a pile of rags, something to be discarded, Anna could feel her faith in humanity evaporate, this just couldn't be. Despite her experience with this monster she had somehow believed that he wouldn't be capable of anything more than happened to her. The conclusion of his terrorisation of her didn't occur, thus her mind didn't see beyond it. She, of all people knew that some humans were capable of the most atrocious acts against one another, in her line of work, to the most vulnerable, to children. But this?

Her nausea increased and she ran to the kitchen sink, retching until there was nothing left inside her, turning on the taps and splashing her face with cold water she caught her reflection in the kitchen window. Snippets from her past seemed to emerge in her battered mind, the morality, strength, fortitude that her parents had instilled in her was reasserted. They wouldn't expect her to crumble. They would expect her to do the right thing, to dig deep and face this horror head on. She could do this, this animal needed to be behind bars for the rest of his life and each and every victim needed to be heard.

With a face drained of all colour and eyes as wide and glazed as a deer caught in headlights, she returned to the living room to watch the remaining DVD's.

* * *

By dawn the floor was scattered with DVD boxes, each one had been viewed. Surveying the litter of boxes she vaguely realised that neither she nor Charlie had appeared on any of the DVD's, if he had filmed her and Charlie at all it wasn't here, she no longer cared, in the scheme of things she had just witnessed her very own sex tape just seemed pathetic, mundane. She had suspected as much, the point of this was not to live up to his end of the bargain, it was to assault her, to finish the job psychologically where he had failed physically. To a degree, he had succeeded. Anna knew that a part of her had died on this night, would never return. The part of her that believed in the capacity for change, for rehabilitation, in that glimmer that all humans have but would take one cathartic moment for another to crack the shell and allow the humanity to seep in, slowly but surely filling the veins. She didn't believe in God or the Devil but she now believed that evil existed. A thousand difficult and abusive childhoods could not explain what she had witnessed on her TV screen. A sense of horror pervaded her being like the tentacles of a malevolent beast. They writhed and slithered into her very nerve endings, causing involuntary shudders. But above all of this and to her surprise she retained her sense of justice, of doing what was right, making sure that this monster would never be free to commit these acts again. She had made her deal with him knowing she wouldn't fulfil her end of the bargain. It was a game, an unholy dance, now he would face the consequences of his actions. He might be sat in his cell with a smug, arrogant grin on his face at the moment, but this would fade with time, he would realise that his arrogance had got the better of him. She picked up her phone and called DI Cooper.

* * *

She immediately realised that the call to the Detective Inspector was inappropriate, it was six forty five in the morning. He was probably still in bed, asleep. A sleep oblivious to the hurt and pain that had a few moments ago emanated from her TV screen. A third ring, she was about to hang up, phone now in her lap, finger on the red handset. "Andy speaking" A voice robotic, clearly he had been woken from his slumber by a ringing phone many times before. "Hi, DI Cooper, It's Anna Black." Her voice was faltering, faltering because of the time she was calling, because of the images that were imprinted behind her eyes, because she was scared, tired. "I'm, I'm sorry, it's still technically night time. I'll call you later." She could hear some muffled shuffling, footsteps, he was leaving his bedroom to take the call elsewhere, not wanting to disturb his partner, no doubt. "It's fine Anna, no problem. Are you OK?" "Yes, just about. I could do with speaking to you, as soon as possible really. I have some evidence of Dave Cartwright's previous crimes, on DVD, here in my living room. Would you be able to come over, get them out of here." She was attempting calm, composed, in her head she sounded dead, a ghost, conveying unintelligible messages over a phone line. Miraculously he understood. No questions, a simple "Yes, of course, it'll take me a couple of hours but I'll be with you as soon as I can. Don't go anywhere, I'll be there soon." The line died, a monotonous, aching tone, she sat and looked at the mobile in her hand. Over the course of the next couple of hours Anna's mind played over incidents in her life, good and bad. The events that had led her to become who she was now. The strong, resilient, loving family, the bad relationships, the good friends, good times, death, happiness, loss. A memory flooded back to her. In the park with her father, he had pushed her so high on a swing that she believed she would launch into the air, She whooped with the exhilaration of it, head back, viewing the upside down image of her father, smiling at her, good times. On their way home from the park Anna noticed a flutter of wings in a small gathering of trees. She let go of her father's hand and ran towards the flutter, hoping to catch a bird indulging in a dirt bath. She had expected the bird to fly away as she approached, it didn't. This caused her to hesitate, instinctively understanding that something must be wrong. Her father followed her, on seeing the bird he kneeled on the grass at its side. "What's wrong with it daddy?" His face looked a little sad, he reached out and gathered the fluttering bird in a huge hand. One of it's wings was at an odd angle and there was a small drop of blood on the breast of the bird. "It may have been a cat, a fox, I'm not sure Anna. This little fella came off worse I'm afraid." He stroked it's breast with his forefinger, attempting to calm the panicked bird. Father and daughter were still and quiet for some time, both affected to varying degrees by the plight of the bird. It had calmed somewhat, it's tiny heart beat visible on it's breast and then the beating stopped. The eyes glazed, head flopping onto her father's palm. The child Anna began to cry, "Is the bird dead daddy?" Her father turned to look at her. "Yes, he's dead Anna, did you not see him fly away?" She was puzzled. A shake of the head "What do you mean, he's there in your hand." her tears were now ebbing in favour of the curiosity she had for her father's statement. "Your right in a way. His body is in my hand, but it's nothing more than just a few feathers and bones, the thing that kept him alive flew away." He looked around and saw three or four birds in a nearby tree. "He went that way I believe, perhaps he knows the birds up there?" Her father stared at the birds with an intensity and longing that at once unnerved her and made her feel secure at the same time. She was merely seven years old, she couldn't have understood the meaning her father was attempting to convey, yet she was happy to accept the idea that the bird had simply flown away, was reborn.

She had applied this principle to many situations in her life, from actually death, loss, whilst not a Christian she was open minded, maybe there was something out there, a better place, a promotion. She also viewed the difficult situations, people, relationships she had to deal with on an all too regular basis, as a trial, to enter, endure, and to become reborn at the end of the process, a stronger, more resilient individual. Her father had taught her a great lesson and she had never been more grateful for it than she was now.

By the time DI Cooper rang her doorbell Anna was composed, she was calm, able to invite him in and discuss the events of the previous hours. He sat in her blue, what she believed to be cosy, although others disagreed, armchair, listened to her intently, didn't distract her by writing notes, rarely asking questions.

She admitted to him that Dave had made a deal with her. He had given her the code to the lock up and safe, had requested that she obtain and watch the DVD's and then meet with him again. She would have to describe each DVD, if he were convinced that she had done this he would admit to his horrific crimes, if she hadn't, two things. He had warned her that he had someone on the outside, one of his loyal customers who had a vested interest in his "art". He was watching, her, knew who she was, where she lived and when she was going to visit the lock up. If things didn't go exactly to plan he would make sure that his associate "permanently dealt with the issue". Head down, embarrassed by the following selfish reason that she didn't inform the police Anna told of the potential sex tape. Again Dave had embellished the threat, a YouTube, Facebook, Twitter, Yammer expose. Of course, the customer would publish this at Dave's request. Anna admitted to the DI that she wasn't entirely convinced of the second person's existence, but didn't feel she could take the chance. She wanted to get the evidence, wanted to make sure there was enough on this guy to make sure he was given a sentence of "life without parole".

Cooper had listened to all of this intently, he was both in admiration at Ann's fearless attempts to obtain evidence, and conversely annoyed that may have contaminated it. She wouldn't have worn latex gloves, may have smudged vital prints. All of the small, yet, contributory factors that resulted in convictions. Philosophically, he determined he would focus his appraisal of Anna with his first thought, she was brave, she was trying to do the right thing.

"Right, so I think Anna, what we need is a plan, do you agree?" She nodded, a little too eagerly, giving the impression that she wanted to hand over responsibility of this nightmare to someone else. That assumption was wrong, what she wanted was a resolution." I'm going to get the SOCO's over to retrieve these discs, I'll also get them over to the lockup, I need the details, do you still have them?" Another nod, "I'll write down the location and code for you. There were cassettes in the safe, lots of them, you know, VHS cassettes." He nodded.

"Now this is the big question Anna, do you want to go back to speak with him?" A long silence. She sighed "First, I want to know that you have enough evidence on the tapes alone to convict him. I think you will, he wears a mask in some of them but in others, and for parts of the films where he wears it, you can identify who he is, well I could anyway." She leaned across to the coffee table and strained a magazine, a nervous, absent minded gesture. "He just wants to mess me up, you know? I need to put this behind me, get the upper hand." She shook her head and laughed.

"That sounds really arrogant doesn't it? That's not what I mean, I want him to understand that he doesn't have any control over me. I don't believe he has "someone on the outside" as he put it, that doesn't worry me. What worries me if that I don't get this worm that he has managed to get inside of my head out now, while I have the opportunity, I'll never get rid of it. That scares me DI Cooper, really scares me."

"Two things Anna, its Andy and you're a very brave woman." He smiled at her, his face changing quite dramatically from a pensive, determine expression to one that grandchildren would have been drawn to, like moths to a flame, warm, benevolent and kind. "I suggest you contact your boyfriend, get him over here, he'll be worried about you. In the meantime we'll conduct our investigations and I'll let you know the outcome. It shouldn't take too long to determine whether or not the DVD's will be enough." Cooper was aware that a couple of DVD's was not going to make the case, but he did know that it would give him an indication of whether or not he would have to ask her to wear a wire in her confrontation with Cartwright. This woman needed closure, and the sooner the better, she had clearly been pretty together before this nightmare had begun, he didn't want that undoing by a bad, bad man. There needed to be at least one person who wasn't a casualty of David Cartwright.

Chapter Thirty-five

The second time in a week that she had been sat in the waiting room of the prison. This time she felt more self-assured, more confident. She glanced around at the other people waiting to see a loved one. Taking it all in, some laughing, joking, the occasional admonishment to a child for straying to far from the protection or control of their parent, mainly women, of varying guises. She was actually surprised by the variety of individuals that had incarcerated partners, family members. She was reminded of a driving course she had been to. An afternoon with a particularly arrogant duo, Mike and Phil. They had been the alternative to three points on her driving license. She had expected a room full of boy racers, middle aged lorry drivers and was surprised to find that three quarters of the participants were beautifully coiffured and made up middle aged women. So much for stereotypes. A small child, maybe two or three years old chased a toy car that came to a resting place at her feet. The child, a boy, stood when he had retrieved the car and looked her square in the face. His cheeks were ruddy and he had large blue eyes, he held up the toy car in front of him "Ca, ca" Anna leaned in towards him "Yes, car sweetie, brum, brum" The little boy laughed and ran back in the direction of who Anna assumed to be his mother. A young woman, in her mid-twenties, the boy ran towards her and launched himself against her knees. The woman looked down at him, with a sad face, she ruffled his hair and drew him to her, whispering something in his ear. All the while a faraway look in her eyes, probably trying to work out how she had gotten into this position, her boy having to visit his father in prison, life shouldn't have turned out like this. What went wrong?

"Anna Black?" was it the same guard who had nonchalantly disregarded her on her previous visit? She wasn't sure, but it didn't matter, she was about to face her demon. This would require all of her concentration, all of her resolve. Sexist guards were small fry compared to this. She stood up, smoothing down the fronts of her trousers as if attempting to preen herself before a visit to a seldom seen lover. She followed the guard into the visiting room and was overcome with a sense of déjà vu. Dave was sat at the same table as before, again checking out his fingernails, this time she was very aware that he knew she had walked through the door, he was feigning nonchalance. She knew that this was going to be his last moment of glory, the final person outside of a prison cell that he could destroy, his finale. She had the upper hand. A call from Cooper yesterday had provided her with some relatively good news. It seemed that Mr Dave Cartwright had a small, but incredibly unique birthmark on his shoulder blade. The birthmark made several appearances in Dave's films, and had given Anna what she needed to confront this demon and then lay to rest this traumatic episode of her life.

Striding across the hall she pulled out the chair opposite to him, unwilling to allow him any control over the conversation, making her stance before he had the chance to do so she said "So, I'm here, I watched the films. Not sure what you want me to say? Bad editing, mediocre sound tracks, no sex tape that I was in. Not that the kind of sex I indulge in holds any interest for today's market, certainly not for your market." It was her turn to absently check out the quality of her nails. She didn't look up, wouldn't look at him, she was hoping he was shocked, thrown, caught off guard. "So the deal was, I watched the, erm...films and you confessed to the crimes." Now she focused on him, she was right to assume he would be shocked, this was throwing his world upside down. A female calling the shots, being as unemotional as you'd like. His expression was a snapshot that Anna would forever hold in her mind when she deliberated this whole, awful mess. He was in melt down, his eyes reflected the fact that his brain was not computing what was happening. She almost felt sorry for him, slack jawed and confusion in his eyes. Was it this easy? Surely not, she had braced herself for a psychological punch up. If this was it she may be as disappointed as he was.

He bowed his head onto the table, large hands smoothing his hair and tucking it behind his ears. A new face emerged, the same sickening grin she had seen before. "You're good Anna, you had me there for a moment. Seriously, you're good" A drawn out, thick attempt at a laugh. "Really? Erm, thanks, but not quite sure what you mean Dave, I'd like to ask in what way I'm "good" but the fact is I have other things to do, important things. Do you want to confess to one of the police officers? I'm assuming you will confess, I take it you're a man of your word?"

"I'm a man of my word alright Anna, yes. But of course I wanted to confess to you, to you Anna not to them, the coppers. You know what I'm thinking don't you?" His intense gaze, suddenly earnest, willing her to be drawn in, she suppressed a shudder "Go on Dave." A less authoritarian edge to her voice, the tables slowly turning. "I believe that you and I are kindred spirits, we occupy opposite ends of the spectrum, granted, but we are essentially the same." Anna sat with intense look on her face, nodding at Dave as he spoke. She realised he would continue this monologue, it wasn't at all for her benefit, more to feed his ego and justify the warped perception he had of reality. But the confession, she needed to sit through this, just in case. There was a possibility that he would tell her more. She had to see this thing through, grit your teeth Anna. "I can agree with you, we are opposite sides of the coin, but that's not why I'm here Dave, is it?"

She tapped her nails in a rhythmic motion on the table in front of her, from little to fore finger, all the while staring at Dave, an unreadable expression on her face. "I did what you asked me to do, now what do you have to tell me? In about thirty minutes I'm going to walk out of here, and I probably won't ever come back, so if you're going to tell me something of value, do it. If not save us both the time and I'll get out of here." Dave had been looking at Anna while she spoke, gave him her commands, there was curious expression on his face, amusement, incredulity, she wasn't sure. Whatever he was feeling, it did the trick. "It all started with my mother, so called mother that is. She was nothing more than a fucking whore that was taking up oxygen, do you know what I mean?"

Anna nodded and then sat through the grim confessions of an extremely damaged individual. He told her enough, she would be able to direct DI Cooper to the remains of at least three more victims. Her stomach was churning and her head was threatening a headache. She realised she had enough information, in addition to the videos, this guy was going nowhere. She refocused on his words. "So you see Anna, how alike we are?" Her face screwed up into something unrecognisable so disturbed was she that this connection would even entered the diseased man's head. "Dave, Dave, I'm going to have to stop you there. Two things. We are not the same, in no way, shape or form, your fucking nuts, evil, I actually don't give a shit, mad or bad you're a pollution on this society, and secondly, I am not going to be spending the rest of my days in prison, same food, same conversations, same four walls, no holidays, no more film making, do you know what I'm saying Dave? You're a fucking caged animal, in a zoo. And guess what? I'm not. Did you think you were going to destroy me by asking me to watch those DVD's? Really, are you so caught up in your own delusions that you think you're the only one. Dave, I work in child protection, how many of the likes of you do I come across in a month, no, a week, you're ten a penny, nothing unusual. It's my bread and butter, if it wasn't for people like you I wouldn't have a job!" Anna laughed at him, really at him and she could see his demeanour changing yet again. His blood was boiling, a scarlet rash appeared above his prison issue polo shirt and continued to rise, clawing its way into his cheeks. His fists were clenched like Thor's hammers on the table before him. If he had raised them to leave an indentation she wouldn't have been surprised. Anna realised it was time for her to leave. "Thanks for the info Dave, I'll be sure to pass it on to Cooper." She stood, and nodded to a nearby guard. This was how she wanted to leave him, furious, unable to resolve the exchange that had taken place, unable to rein her in, control her. Wanting to glance down at him for the last time, resisting as she knew that her ignorance of him would further infuriate and harm him, she marched out of the visiting room in the same manner that she had marched in, victorious.

Chapter Thirty-six

A couple of phone calls had determined that the agency job was still vacant, the manager had decided that Anna was welcome back if she so wished. Desperate times called for desperate measures. Anna glanced at her reflection in the bathroom mirror. A fleeting thought, was this the same person looking back at her that had stood in the same spot, brushing her teeth in the same was as this doppelganger? She felt not. The stranger starring at her intently had colder eyes, a deeper frown, changed in some way, subtle but noticeable. She shook her head, tearing away from the stare. She could contemplate the minutiae later, but now, now she had the impossible task of slotting herself back into normality, a job, then a life. A date with Charlie this evening. He had been a rock, had supported her through this ordeal and she was grateful. She could feel herself falling for him and didn't quite know if it was Charlie himself or the role he had played that she was falling for. Perhaps a little of both. Whatever, the most important decision she had to make right now was what to wear, formal, informal. Why had these intrinsic decisions suddenly become so difficult to make, what the hell did it matter? She admonished herself for being so ridiculous and chose an outfit that she would normally wear for work, a pair of grey trousers and a black tailored shirt. How difficult was that Anna? Internal dialogue, louder in her head these past few weeks, parenting her, maintaining her sanity. Just trying to find her way, get through this. The goal was in sight, job, work, normality, hold on Anna. An hour later she was back in the new office, the job that had almost been. The manager was there to welcome her, the smile and enthusiasm not quite as larger than life as the first time around. Anna felt an explanation was in order, she didn't want to appear like some kind of flaky histrionic.

Cindy sat, contemplating Anna's revelations, which had been a brief synopsis of the last few months. It was clearly enough for Cindy to appreciate the trauma that Anna had suffered and she was shocked by harsh reality. "You sure you're ready to get back to work? Seriously Anna, maybe you need some time to, erm, process?"

Anna smiled "If I wasn't ready for work then I wouldn't be here. Can I be frank Cindy? This is strictly between you and me, I don't want other workers knowing about this. I need to normalise, get back to work, do the job that I know how to do. I have something to offer, I assume that's why you hired me in the first place, nothing's changed.

"OK, let's get you to work then, yeah?" Anna made a curious face, an expression Anna couldn't quite grasp. It didn't matter, she wanted a case, something to take her mind far, far away from Cartwright."

* * *

Anna dropped the paper file onto her desk with an audible thunk. There were a couple of people in the office, looking up with a smile and a nod, then faces turned busily to their monitor screens. Not the friendliest, she didn't care, the last thing she wanted was congenial chatter about her work history.

Cindy had informed Anna that the most pressing case had an electronic file, but the history was contained within a paper file, as it had not yet been uploaded, overworked admin. Anna starred at the manila folder that took up the space of at least a quarter of the small desk. The front had a name and a date, Paige Connor, 01.10.1987.

A read though risk assessments, initial assessments, minutes of meetings, visit recordings painted a very sad picture. Paige had been a normal child, had friends, had apparently loved her family, no issues. Had obtained several "O" levels, a couple of "A" levels, commenced a University course in Humanities. Paige appeared to be doing quite well, her family had stated that occasionally she would get down and would retreat, not physically it would seem but mentally, disengaging from those around her. They believed this was how she dealt with pressure and supported her through these episodes, a few days and she was fine. Other than this, nothing remarkable. Second year of University Paige is the victim of a suspected "date rape" She goes out for a few drinks with a couple of her friends, nothing heavy, it's Wednesday, a pound a bottle at the student union bar. Friends report that they chatted about an assignment that needed handing in by Friday, Paige as ever was on the ball, had completed it. They all mingled with the other students at the bar. Paige began to act a little strange, intoxicated beyond the couple of beers she had consumed. She had decided to go home. Paige doesn't remember going home or the rest of the evening, just waking late the following day with a pulsing headache and a feeling of panic. Shortly after this she became paranoid, acting in a bizarre manner, a diagnosis of schizophrenia was stamped on her forehead and she discovered she was pregnant. Anna presumed the child in question was a result of the rape.

An awful story, the poor girl had clearly been through hell, but she had some support. The family were involved and Paige attended a local church, there was some kind of network around her. It was somewhere for Anna to start. Despite the tragic tale she had just read, Anna smiled. She really was glad to be back at work. She had hoped that forcing some structure and normality into her life would create structure and normality. It appeared to have worked. Not yet lunchtime and she already had her work head on. All others thoughts had been squeezed out of her mind. She realised that everything was going to be alright.

* * *

"So, how did it go?" Charlie was pouring a glass of red wine, he handed it to Anna, watching her from the corner of his eye. "It was fine. Would you believe the first case I picked up has child protection stuff?" A small, ironic laugh. "Really, what case? I had a mental health case wedged in my pigeon hole today." Anna laughed "Well, that would be some kind of a coincidence! Paige Connor is mum's name..." "Are you serious?" Charlie was incredulous. His shocked expression melted very quickly to concern, "Is this a conflict of interests?"

"Oh God Charlie! You sound like me! Sit down and drink your wine." Charlie did as he was told, a smile creased his cheeks and they both erupted into laughter. Everything was going to be ok.

Printed in Great Britain
by Amazon.co.uk, Ltd.,
Marston Gate.